NATIVE BLOOD

BOOK 1 ZEB HANKS MYSTERY SERIES

MARK REPS

This book is a work of fiction. Names and characters are products of the author's imagination. Any similarities between the good people of southeastern Arizona and tribal members of the San Carlos Indian Reservation are purely coincidental.

NATIVE BLOOD

ACKNOWLEDGMENTS

A writer is much like a sheriff. His work defines him and the buck stops with him. However, it is the people who support him that really determine the final outcome.

Over the last 30 years I have continually visited Graham County and the San Carlos Reservation. With each passing year, I find the people to be more and more welcoming as I learn more about the area, hear more local stories and interact with those who have lived in the area their entire lives. I would like to heartily thank the people of Graham County and the San Carlos Reservation.

I must acknowledge my wife, Kathy, who is indefatigable in putting up with me when I get lost in the process of writing. She also lets me know when my writing is getting off the rails and edits with minimal complaining.

T he driver tapped a solitary fingertip against the face of his watch. His heart drummed a taut, slightly anxious beat against his sternum. Thirteen minutes of deafening silence was beginning to erode his confidence. Reaching across the car seat, he placed his hand on his Coleman cooler. Self-assurance returned. Clarity of thought returned. Calm logic followed. He breathed easily.

Stopping the car in the middle of the dirt road, he methodically shifted the T-bar into park. He yanked the keys from the ignition, grabbed a flashlight from the glove compartment and stepped out into the open night air. The blackness surrounding him further eased the pressure in his head.

A rattlesnake, sliding through the edges of the hardened road rut, stopped to hiss at him. Using the heel of his boot, he thrust an uncoordinated kick at its head. It slithered off into the underbrush, rattling its tail. He hurled a ball of spit in its direction as he stared at the rear of the car.

"Goddamn bitch kicked out a tail light."

In the darkness, he fumbled with the key until the trunk popped open. He clicked the flashlight on. He held it above his head. The bright rays shined on the young girl's face. She didn't move. His eyes jumped to her all too flaccid features. Her lids rested smoothly over her eyes. There was no sign of life. He placed his fingers on the side of her neck to check for a pulse. The trunk smelled of dust, sweat and oil. She was warm. He growled under his breath.

"Goddamn it."

He pulled the duct tape from her mouth to give her room to breathe. He jammed his finger into her mouth, checking to see if he bound her so tightly that she might have swallowed her tongue. She hadn't. Momentary relief. If she was dead, his years of planning were for nothing. Softly caressing her cheek with the back of his hand, he pleaded with her.

"Come on, baby. Give me a sign. Show me what you're made of."

She didn't budge. Not the merest hint of life was present. He pressed his thumb over her eyelid. Softly at first, then with heavy pressure. She emitted a muffled cry of exquisite agony.

"Stupid bitch! Playing possum on me. That's disrespectin' me. Huge mistake."

He slid his hand around her throat and pressed down hard enough to make her gag. She choked out a gurgled plea for him to stop.

"I could snap your neck in two seconds flat, you dirty little scumbag. You are lucky, damn lucky that I am a patient man."

He slammed the trunk down hard and kicked the rear bumper, twice.

"I oughta kill you for wreckin' the tail light. This Mustang is a collector's item," he shouted.

Her fruitless struggling began anew as he got back behind the wheel, continuing to his final destination. The vanity of her hopeless efforts sent an orgasmic tingling through his body. His head felt electric. He began to hum a favorite tune, one his father sang to him when he was falling asleep as a child. He ran his tongue over the inside of his lips. The sensual feeling excited him. The soft hum from the back of his throat became a sweet serenade as he neared his destination.

"Hush little baby, don't you cry. Papa's gonna sing you a lullaby."

When he turned off the car, the movement in the trunk ceased. He sneered, banged a fist on the dashboard and shouted.

"We're here. I know you're still in there. It's not nice to play dead."

Grabbing a knapsack from the back seat, he flipped on the overhead light. He quickly inventoried what he had packed. Candles, matches, razor knife, abalone shell, latex gloves, surgical scissors, sewing kit, ceremonial dress—all present and accounted for. He placed the sack next to a cooler of dry ice. Lingering momentarily, he caressed the lid with his fingertips.

Outside the car, he paused to gaze heavenward. In the million stars shining in the sky, he saw the divine face of his father smiling down on him. The desert winds carried a whispering voice that coaxed, "take her, take her, she's yours."

He pulled his quarry from the trunk. He made certain not to hit her head on the hard metal, not for her sake but for the sake of his collector's item, the Mustang. A lone coyote in the distance howled mournfully as he carried her to the natural rock outcropping he had preordained as an altar.

"Lie still and you'll be fine," he said. "Your job is so easy. Mine is difficult. Just follow my orders."

As he slowly removed her dress, a silent stream of tears came rushing from the corners of her eyes, creating a watery trail over her flushed cheeks. The fluttering wings of a nighthawk as it swooped upon its hapless prey echoed in the small canyon behind him.

Taking a clean, white handkerchief from a pocket, he softly

brushed away the wetness from her face. She jerked her head away from his touch and fought to utter something through the sticky tape. He placed a finger gently on the tape over her lips, shushing her. His voice became that of a balladeer as he sang softly, sweetly.

"Hush little darlin' don't say a word. Papa's gonna buy you a mockingbird."

She watched through terrified eyes as the surgical gloves slipped easily over his slender fingers. Her tears froze as his pure white hands reached into the knapsack. The young girl panicked and began to struggle violently as he held a knife above her head. On this moonless night, its razor-sharp blade reflected a thousand stars. The starlight danced chaotically on the finely honed metal. Her eyes begged for mercy. No such emotion existed in the killer's heart.

Freeing herself just enough to land a hard kick of her knees to his groin, the young woman's hope rose, if only momentarily, as she watched the pain on her captor's face. The knife slipped from his taught grip and drifted through the air in slow motion. She dug deep to find enough strength to torque her neck. She felt the falling tip of the blade as it grazed against her throat before piercing the ground. He pressed the force of his body weight against her. With hot, angry breath he whispered in her ear.

"Don't move, bitch. And that's the last time I'm going to tell you."

Her muscles remained tense but she obeyed. She didn't cry, didn't even flinch until he pressed the tip of the blade against her soft belly. Suddenly and ferociously, her survival instinct demanded action. She battled with what little remaining strength her body could muster. But the challenge against his superior strength as he pinned her against the rocks and dirt was utterly pointless.

"I said don't fight."

A nighthawk flying overhead screeched out a wailing cry. Its prey yielded, uttering a dying plea.

He placed one hand beneath her head and brought her forehead to his lips. The night became silent. As he kissed her, he drew the scalpel's honed edge through her skin. The resistance was no more than the surface of a ripe peach offers to a sharp knife.

"Now you get what's coming," he said.

She heaved up violently as he began the process of cutting her heart from her chest. She gasped wordlessly beneath the gag. Her spine buckled with a jerk as blood drooled from her mouth beneath the duct tape. Her eyes rolled up, disappearing into her skull. Her shaking body's final upsurge shook all remaining life from her being. All movement ceased. Her final exhalation drifted away on the desert wind.

The killer smiled serenely as he went to work. He placed the heart in the Coleman cooler next to the dry ice. The etched abalone shell was positioned where her heart had been. He proceeded to use the sewing kit to close the wounds he had inflicted with the surgical knife. Smiling, he placed her in the ceremonial dress. It was all so easy, so right, so erotic. Carefully, he placed the candles around her at the four directions. The perfect touch, he thought. Removing the latex gloves, he placed them in his bag. He lit the candles. In the still of the night, they barely fluttered. Finally, he looked around making certain he left nothing other than what he intended. Once again, he began his fateful hymn.

"And if that mocking bird don't sing, Papa's gonna buy you a diamond ring. And if that diamond ring turns brass, Papa's gonna buy you a looking glass."

He smiled, rejoicing in the execution of his plan.

2

Z eb Hanks, Graham County Sheriff, detested sitting behind a desk. When he returned to Safford after a stint as a Tucson policeman, he never imagined being overwhelmed with the same level of paperwork that drove him from the big city bureaucracy. Each new governmental form, each new rule and regulation, seemed to carry him further and further away from the job he signed up for, to serve and protect the citizens of Graham County.

At six feet three inches and two hundred thirty pounds, he was too large for the government-issued chair. His legs cramped so tightly beneath the old wooden desk that a frequent passing thought had him imagining how tight a coffin must feel.

Gripping a number two pencil between his slab thick fingers, he monotonously tapped a cadence with the rubber eraser against his daily calendar and stared out the window. Outside a pair of red tail hawks glided atop the mid-morning thermals. Odd, he thought, flying so closely together this early in the day and away from mating season. As a child, he had learned from the old Apaches who gathered in the town park that such anomalies were omens, harbingers of bad luck. His dad had sneered at the idea. Such talk was hogwash from the preachy mouths of half-witted drunks.

The hawks quickly vanished from sight. Zeb's eyes turned to a pile of paperwork resting atop his calendar. Running an idle finger across the four corners that boxed in the day's date, October 18, Zeb silently repeated the date in his mind. October eighteenth, it meant something. But what was so important about October eighteenth? More importantly, why couldn't he remember? Zeb chastised himself for his failing memory.

"Helen," he shouted. "Could you step in here for a minute? I've got a question."

Helen Nazelrod abruptly stopped her typing, pushed herself away from her secretarial desk, snorted not too discreetly through her nose and marched into the sheriff's office. This type of interruption, part of the normal ebb and flow of working for Zeb, made her miss her former boss, Sheriff Jake Dablo. At least Jake Dablo had the courtesy not to shout. The new sheriff seemed to have left his manners in the big city.

"Something about October eighteenth is stuck in my craw, and I can't jar it loose. I can't remember for the life of me what it is about today that's so important. Got any ideas?"

The sinewy Helen, hair wrapped tightly in a bun, was significantly more than a secretary to the sheriff's department. A faithful county employee for over thirty years, the sixty-year-old Helen knew the system, how it worked, where the skeletons were buried and who shoveled the dirt. But her job description didn't include being Zeb's memory. Whereas some people forget things over time, Helen's recall only became more acutely tuned. She publicly credited a preserved mind and a healthy body to the lifestyle coincident with being a strict Mormon. No alcohol or tobacco had ever passed her lips and none ever would. She believed a healthy diet of fresh fruits and vegetables combined with community service and daily prayer could do the same for anyone's memory.

Zeb, who mostly dined on burgers, bacon, eggs and chili, was irregular at Sunday service and prayed only when prompted. He was less grateful for Helen's devotion to her faith than to her unflagging memory.

"The 18ᵗʰ of October 1992. Seven years ago today Sheriff Dablo's granddaughter, Angel, was murdered."

The tone was that of a scolding school marm. She may as well have added, "How could you have forgotten?" Her sullen facial expression and the objection from her steely gray eyes said it for her. Sheriff Hanks inspected the tips of his boots like a chastened child. How *could* he have forgotten this date? It was the day Safford had lost its innocence, a day that produced the darkest blemish ever on the collective soul of Graham County.

The years on the street beat in Tucson had taught Zeb to bury the personal side of murder. Solved or unsolved, murder cases all had the same finality, pieces of paper jammed into a cold, metal cabinet. But Angel's murder was different. Angel was the grandchild of Jake Dablo, the man who was his hero as well as his mentor.

Helen stood stiffly in front of the sheriff's oak desk, steno pad in hand, awaiting his return gaze. It was slow in coming.

"Anything else?" she asked.

Her voice dripped with disdain. As he looked up, Sheriff Hanks' face carried the look of a whipped puppy.

"I'm sorry."

His hushed voice was barely audible.

"Sorry?" she whispered inquiringly. "Sorry?"

"I'm sorry I forgot the importance of October eighteenth. For Sheriff Dablo's and his family's sake none of the citizens of Graham County should ever forget this date."

Sheepishly rolling the pencil between his thumb and finger, he let it dribble over the date.

"I'm sorry too," replied Helen. "I'm sorry any of us have to remember. I'm sorry that none of us ever forgets. And it grieves me to no end that the devil didn't bypass Graham County that night seven years ago."

Helen exited the office, leaving the door slightly ajar, true to her habit. A moment later a gust of warm wind slammed it shut. The sheriff leaned back in his chair. Placing his hands on top of a thick, black head of hair, he brought the heels of his well-worn but freshly polished boots to his desktop. The horrible events attached to the date of October eighteenth came crashing through his memory bank with the reckless abandon of water cascading through a flooded canyon on the heels of a spring thaw. Remembering heinous deeds was more than he wanted to deal with today, or any day for that matter. But the runaway train of recollection had been set in unstoppable motion as detail after detail returned, carrying with them long repressed images. Closing his eyes only brought greater clarity to the curse of memory.

He grabbed his old cowboy hat and pressed it against his chest. His memory brought back the child's face, the innocent countenance of a dead little girl. It was seared into his memory. Etched in his mind alongside the dead girl's image was that of her grandfather's face, dour and forever broken. At the time of the murder, his return to Safford was only months old. He could leave the ghosts of the anonymous dead in Tucson. But here in Safford, his home town, the worst of all worlds lay beneath his feet, hidden in the ever-shifting desert sands. He knew from experience that when children died, theirs was not the only soul that departed the earth.

Sheriff Hanks gazed out the window overlooking the center of his hometown. He eyes fell upon the ancient cottonwood tree in the courtyard. Here, Jimmy Song Bird had explained how *true* Apaches never spoke the name of the dead. To this day, even though he believed it merely an old Apache superstition, Zeb avoided saying the name of Angel Bright. To this day, neither the name of Angel Bright nor that of her mother was mentioned by even non-Apaches. But at this moment, something was different. A touch of evil permeated the air.

"Angel, Angel Bright," he said softly. "A bright angel, now in heaven."

A hundred miles beyond the ancient cottonwood sat the city of Tucson and an open invitation for a return to his old job. At least in the city ghosts didn't have names or, worse, personal history.

"Angel Bright."

His words caused a spasm in the pit of his stomach. The sheriff suddenly found himself needing something extremely ordinary to make this a normal day. Serving a writ or two, even a humorous encounter with Fritz, the town drunk, or finding Joe Black Feathers' one eyed dog wandering through the alleyway would do just fine. But wishing away reality has the unintended consequence of drawing it ever nearer.

Helen knocked twice sharply on his door. The sheriff's feet dropped to the hardwood floor as his secretary entered. He pulled the cowboy hat away from his heart and placed it on the desk.

"Sheriff, it's that man, Eskadi Black Robes, from the San Carlos Reservation on the phone. He's demanding to talk to you."

Zeb took a deep breath and blew it out hard between tightly pursed lips. This day was going downhill in a hurry.

"Eskadi Black Robes?" What does he want with me?"

"He didn't say. You want me to ask Mr. Black Robes for you?"

"No. No, I'll take it. You sure he didn't say what he wanted to talk about?"

"How long have I been doing this job, Sheriff?"

She paused for less than a fraction of a second before answering her own question.

"Thirty-one years next April. If Eskadi Black Robes would have said what he wanted, I would tell you."

"Sorry, Helen."

Helen, making no bones about the level of her disgust, gave Sheriff Hanks a good, old-fashioned Mormon up and down, stopping at his eyes, saying nothing. He had witnessed enough of her behavior over the years to know what her cold gaze meant. She was forgiving him because of his bad day, but he'd better snap to, pronto!

"Would you please shut the door for me, Helen?" asked the sheriff.

Helen quietly semi-closed the door. Zeb, chewing away at an irritating hangnail, glared at the phone. What could Eskadi Black Robes want from him? Since becoming a tribal official on the San Carlos, Black Robes had all but shunned interaction with the White community. Eskadi's ardent belief that there were two separate worlds within one land, and two separate ways of doing things, made him difficult to deal with. The relationship between the San Carlos Apache tribe and local citizens had never been a rosy one. It wasn't uncommon in Zeb's youth for the Indians and Whites to brawl over scarce day labor jobs and practically go to war over the better ones at the copper mines. His own father had spent more than a few nights in the local jail after decking it out with Indians who had crossed him, inflaming his short temper. Zeb remembered his old man saying, more than once, "Those damn Injuns look at me like I don't even have a soul. They can all go to hell for all I give a shit."

Zeb's first memory of Eskadi was of a skinny, nerdy, quiet kid with hand-me-down clothes and oversized glasses. But ever since returning to the reservation from college in California, his politics had become radicalized, and his voice demanded to be heard. It was as if he had swallowed the rattle of and grown the fangs of a nasty, desert diamondback rattler. He had become a genuine, left-wing, off-the-wall dissident, a type not appreciated within the city limits of Safford.

With Eskadi's rising tribal power, his views became the public face of the local Apaches within the White world. The old timers grumbled about his demands over their morning coffee. In their minds there was a single kind of justice that fit his ilk, a razor strop and a quick trip behind the woodshed. Some even suggested a few ounces of lead might do the trick.

Wherever Eskadi went he left behind a trail of discord. Even inside the tribe he was creating friction and infighting. Younger males and educated Apache women who sided with him saw the changes in the power structure as long past due. In their collective thinking change was not happening quickly enough. The Elders disagreed with their progeny, freely pointing out that Eskadi had returned from the White man's world with a chip on his shoulder. The old men and women voiced a strong opinion in favor of a slower, more tempered way of changing the world.

But Eskadi's most recent demands included the return of Apache land and millions of dollars in reparations for land he claimed to have been taken illegally by the government and given to the mining companies. He had publicly been making loud noises about a long history of lies from the Bureau of Indian Affairs. When it came to broken treaties, water rights and repatriation of Apache territory, the federal government was equally to blame. Recently, when their cars passed on the highway, Eskadi hadn't even returned the sheriff's friendly wave. So why in the hell was he calling today?

Sheriff Hanks looked down at the flashing red button on his

phone. Helen noticed the sheriff hadn't picked up yet, turned, looked over her shoulder and peered over the top of her glasses through the slightly open door to see what the holdup was. Feeling the heat of her gaze, the sheriff peered in her direction, raised his eyebrows and nodded. Satisfied, she returned to her paperwork.

"This is Sheriff Hanks."

He snarled his name in his most authoritative tone, knowing full well that it was pointless to approach Eskadi in such a manner. But it was a strange day. Who knew what anyone was thinking? For all he knew Eskadi might have a bug up his ass about a White sheriff arresting one of his tribe. The last time Mormon ranchers' cattle had wandered onto the reservation from nearby Bureau of Land Management property, Eskadi raised a fit. When Zeb tried to reason with him, Eskadi threatened to butcher the cattle and give the meat to his people as partial payment for past sins of the 'imperialistic, invading White skins'. God only knew what he would want this time.

"This is Eskadi Black Robes. Is there any chance your business finds you up towards Antelope Flats today?"

The sheriff moved the phone an arm's length away from his ear and stared at it like he couldn't believe the words he had just heard. What the hell? What the hell was Eskadi talking about? Eskadi would never think, not even for one moment, that the sheriff had business on Apache land. Sheriff Hanks put the phone back to his ear. The silent hum offered nothing in the way of an explanation.

"Antelope Flats is on the San Carlos. That's tribal police jurisdiction, isn't it? Hardly a place for a White skin who might get arrested for trespassing." Zeb's response sounded extremely sarcastic, even to his own ears.

"Yes, it's Native American land, Zebulon. But I would like

you to come up here today if it's at all possible. I mean, if you can find the time. It's rather important."

The sheriff's ears burned in disbelief. Eskadi Black Robes called him Zebulon and asked for help all in the same breath. The two of them had never been on a first name basis, even in childhood. Still stunned by the apparent softening in Eskadi's attitude, Zeb quickly concluded that whatever Eskadi wanted was very serious.

"Are you still there, Zeb?"

Now it was Zeb, not Zebulon.

"Yu-up, I'm still here. I guess I could make my way up there today, if it's that important."

"It is," said Eskadi. "Could you meet me in Bylas, say around noon at the Silver Spur Saloon?"

"That sounds doable. You mind telling me what this is about before I head up there? I don't have a lot of time to waste."

"There's been a murder." Eskadi's voice cracked ever so slightly as he spoke.

Eskadi paused so long after saying murder that the sheriff thought the line had gone dead.

"It happened very late last night or early this morning. The body of a young girl was found out in Antelope Flats. She lived up in Wildhorse Canyon."

"Wildhorse Canyon," said Zeb. "That's where Jimmy Song Bird lives."

"That's why I called you."

Eskadi's answer produced another gripping sensation in Zeb's gut and shot a bilious taste across his lips and tongue.

"It was Song Bird's granddaughter who was murdered."

A lightning bolt shot through Sheriff Hanks's mind unleashing another long-forgotten image. In his mind's eye, Jimmy Song Bird, beautifully dressed in his Apache ceremonial garb with long, shiny, black hair braided in a ponytail hanging to his waist, stood side by side with Jake Dablo. Jake carried the craggy face and timeless visage of a western lawman from a bygone era, only without the holstered gun at his side. That day Jake looked utterly ridiculous in his ill- fitting and seldom worn Sunday suit. Zeb's remembrance was of two good men, Jake Dablo and Jimmy Song Bird, smiling proudly at their daughters' high school graduation, also his graduation.

The girls, Maya Song Bird and Jenny Dablo, were two of the prettiest girls in his graduating class and two of the most troubled. Zeb's heart had carried a hidden schoolboy's crush on at least one of them, and sometimes both, from the time he first started thinking about girls. Much to his dismay, they viewed him only as a friend who sneaked the family car out of the garage late at night to drive around the desert, drink beer and stare at the moon with them.

This day, Jake Dablo and Jimmy Song Bird, who had held their friendship as near and dear as life itself, these men whose lives had been entwined for so long a time, carried a common horrible thread, a link that should join no two men...that of a murdered grandchild. Jake's granddaughter murdered, seven years ago today. And now, on October eighteenth, Jimmy Song Bird's granddaughter had also been taken. The smooth, deep voice of Eskadi Black Robes brought Zeb back from his ugly reflection.

"It looks like a ritualistic murder. Almost identical to Sheriff Dablo's granddaughter a few years back. Only this time the victim is an Apache girl."

Zeb's mind catapulted into disbelief. Only fifteen minutes earlier Helen had dredged up the hideous memory of the murder of Jake's granddaughter. Now, Eskadi invoked the same dead child as well as the murder of a defenseless young Apache child. The most horrific memory in the history of Graham County, a ritualistic mutilation of a child, was repeated seven years later, to the day. Time ground to a screeching halt. The images and thoughts in his mind became more unreal with each passing second. Shaking his head did nothing to clear the thickening haze in the sheriff's mind. The distant mountain and its scrubby undergrowth melded into a single indistinguishable maze. Time somehow doubled back on itself and horrible, vicious memories erupted anew.

"I can be on my way right now. I'll be there in an hour."

"I'll be waiting for you at the Silver Spur."

The sheriff hung up the phone and rubbed a quivering hand through his hair before bringing it to a rest on the nape of his neck. A warm flush followed by an instantly cold, clammy feeling oozed through his skin, leaving his body dampened with beads of icy sweat. A feeling of constriction descending from his throat landed in the pit of his stomach and gripped him like the instant onset of a flu virus. This day was careening from bad to worse. There was no telling what was at the bottom of the ugly abyss that awaited him.

Zeb poured a tall cup of strong, black coffee into a Styrofoam container. He grabbed the keys to the department's Dodge Dakota pickup truck. He stopped momentarily at Helen's desk.

"I'm headed up toward the San Carlos Reservation at the request of Eskadi Black Robes. There's been a murder. A young girl. Up near Antelope Flats. The child was Jimmy Song Bird's granddaughter. You can reach me on the two-way. I'm meeting Eskadi in Bylas. I'll probably be back late. Have Deputy Steele handle anything that comes up in town. Deputy Funke is on rural patrol this morning. He can take care of anything that comes up out in the country. I'm sure you will keep everything else under control."

The door had barely closed behind Zeb when Helen picked up the phone and made the first call, setting in motion a chain of gossip that moved through town faster than a late August wildfire.

Helen called her best friend, who passed it on to the girls at the coffee klatch, who in turn called cousins, sisters, brothers, uncles, aunts—anyone who might possibly be interested in passing on the sad news. By the time supper would be set on the tables in the homes of the small community of Safford, only the town hermits and recluses would be without knowledge of the young girl's murder. By the time the supper hour was over, there would be no shortage of suspects and more than a little finger pointing.

As Helen gossiped, she found herself idly writing the date, October 18, on a blank piece of paper. After tracing over it several times, she underlined it and placed three question marks after the eighteen, underlining them too. Squinting at the exaggerated handwriting, Helen searched her mind. There was something else about the date of October eighteenth. Something she was forgetting. Something she should remember.

3

S heriff Hanks drove a few miles outside the city limits of Safford before removing his hat. When he patrolled local streets, his hat, a symbol of authority, never left his head. As he placed the time worn hat on the seat, he noticed a sweat stain in the shape of a five-cornered badge. The hat carried a long history of its own. It wasn't new when he first placed it on his head. It had been a gift from Jake Dablo. Zeb remembered the day. He was twelve years old, only weeks shy of his thirteenth birthday. Sheriff Jake had come out to the farm that day to arrest his father again. It was the arrest that sent his father to prison where he eventually died. His old man was a drunken thief and a wife beater who hated everyone, especially Apaches. Zeb took another gander at the hat, further dipping into his memories.

That day Jake had tousled his hair. Jake told him to "rest easy" as he placed the hat on young Zeb's head. Sheriff Jake Dablo insisted the hat would be good to him. He told Zeb not to worry, that the world was a big place and things had a way of righting themselves.

"Good always triumphs over evil," Sheriff Jake Dablo told

him with certain authority. The moment Jake placed the cowboy hat on his young head Zeb knew his life had changed forever and for the better.

Zeb didn't cry that day. He wasn't even sad as he watched Jake haul his old man off to jail. Time and circumstance had taught the preteen to hate his father. In Zeb's mind, the sheriff had, in that moment, become his surrogate father. An added benefit was the entrance of Jake's daughter, Jenny Dablo, into his life.

That day was a blessing in so many ways. How many men could point to a single day in their lives, an exact moment, as the pivotal turning point for their future? That day, those events altered the course of Zeb's existence. With the magical placement of an old ten-gallon hat on his head, Jake Dablo had done for Zeb all that a boy could ever ask from a man. He had given him validity.

The road to Bylas also fired the flames of memory regarding Zeb's first meeting with Jimmy Song Bird. It was shortly after Jake had given him the hat. At their first encounter, Song Bird, noting Zeb's deep black hair and pale white skin, baptized him with a sacred Athabascan name. Loosely translated it meant 'Little Sheriff who is both Night and Day'. More importantly, several years later when he was wrestling with a thousand disjointed emotions at the time of his father's death, Song Bird as Medicine Man once again entered his life.

Feeling guilty that he still hated his old man when he died, Zeb's reaction was to raise hell and stay out all night partying with his friends, Maya and Jenny among them. It was at that time Song Bird pulled him aside and explained that he shouldn't hate his father. Zeb's father, Song Bird explained, suffered from an injured spirit, a spirit that could not be healed in his lifetime. He told Zeb that acting out his hatred would do no good for anyone. If he didn't watch himself, he too would damage his own spirit and end up doing evil deeds, perhaps even carrying forward his father's legacy. It was at that moment Zeb was finally able to shed a tear for his departed father.

Zeb observed a pair of scavenging buzzards circle over the rotting carcass of a dead desert animal as he reflected on the hard road of his father's life and the track his own would have taken without the aid of Song Bird and Jake. He shuddered involuntarily.

Zeb's mind turned to murder as his eyes wandered across the vast expanses of the open desert. Song Bird's words about his father's injured soul made him wonder what sort of injury and pain a soul would have to sustain to seek balance by killing a child. It was far easier for him to think about the facts of the murder than to dwell on the underlying motivation of a killer. Zeb was a man hunter, not a psychiatrist. His only goal was to catch the perpetrator of this heinous deed, not to look into the driving forces behind his psyche.

But the thought wouldn't leave him. Where does the pure evil necessary to kill a child come from? And what impels it forward into action? Merely having to think such dark thoughts made Zeb feel tainted and dirty. Spending the trip to Bylas focusing on the evil nature of mankind was getting him nowhere. He cleared his head and regained his grip.

A Peterbuilt semi-tractor trailer zipping by at high speed from the opposite direction produced a wind shear, rattling the Dodge Dakota and practically lifting it off the pavement of State Highway 70. The movement jarred the sheriff away from his inner thoughts and back to a state of present-time consciousness. He checked his speed, seventy-two miles per hour. He would be in Bylas in no time. In Bylas he could begin gathering the facts he needed. Facts were exactly what he would focus on.

Ahead the horizon grew into faintly purple mountain peaks abutting a cloudless blue sky. To the east, jagged tips of land, erupting from beneath the earth's crust millions of years earlier, created a profile like that of an ancient dinosaur spine. Arizona and its ruggedly untamed beauty was made to be loved. But why did God, who created such awesome wonder, also create the soul of a child killer? Why would this evil deed happen out here in this beautiful country? Not once, but twice? Frustrated and caught between beauty and anger, Zeb felt his anger rise.

4

The Silver Spur Saloon was not only the best greasy spoon in Bylas for a cup of coffee, it was the only one. From outside, the cafe could have been mistaken for a time weary tin shed whose structure might be abruptly toppled by a gust from the next Santa Ana wind that blew across the western flatlands. The faded neon Silver Spur Saloon marquee, with only its capital S's remaining actively lit, crackled and groaned on ungreased hinges with minimal coaxing from the gentle breeze.

Sheriff Hanks rolled through the gravel lot and pulled next to the only other vehicle as a flurry of dust swept the parking lot. Returning his hat to his head, he carefully straightened it as he eyed Eskadi Black Robes inside the cafe, hunched forward in a corner booth. His shiny black hair was neatly braided into a waist-length ponytail. He wore wire rimmed glasses and a faded doe skin jacket hunched up around his shoulders. The tribal chairman looked more like a liberal, egghead, college professor than a radical Indian leader. Black Robes didn't turn to acknowledge the sheriff as he entered.

Zeb strutted directly to the booth. Sliding across the cracked leatherette bench, he greeted the tribal leader with a handshake, nearly crushing the other man's fingers. Eskadi slurped his hot coffee and gazed beyond the sheriff, eyeing the clock on the wall and said nothing.

Sitting tall and straight, Zeb towered over Eskadi whose rudeness didn't surprise him. "Eskadi Black Robes," he thought to himself. "I bet it wouldn't take much digging to find an outstanding warrant on the son of a bitch or any of his dirt ball cousins."

A grizzled looking cafe owner with nicotine stained fingers plopped a cup of coffee and plate of doughnuts on the table and departed without saying a word. Still looking beyond Zeb, Eskadi pulled a tape recorder from his jacket.

"I'm sure you won't mind if I make a record of this. I know you can understand the importance of preciseness. I can't believe for a moment that you'll object to me wanting to keep a transcript of what transpires here."

His insolent words brought a hard glare from the lawman's steely eyes. Zeb bit his tongue beneath a curled lip.

"Whatever floats your boat, Chief. Just give it to me straight."

Keeping the small machine tightly gripped in his hand, Eskadi cleared his throat and pressed down the record button.

"About three this morning, maybe a bit earlier, the tribal police got an anonymous tip about a dead body up in Antelope Flats. The caller gave a detailed description of how to find the body, right down to the tenth of a mile to drive on each road, where to turn and hidden landmarks to look for. The dispatcher who answered said the caller most likely was a young, White man. The call was recorded, and I listened to it myself. I can tell you without a doubt, the phone call came from a White."

"If your Apache medicine is so good that you can tell the

color of a man's skin by his voice, maybe you can give me his height, weight, eye color and whether he's been circumcised. While you're at it, why don't you just give me his name and address?"

"No need to get sarcastic with me. As sheriff you must realize that a young White man making an anonymous, middle-of-the-night phone call about the death of an Indian child on remote reservation land begs the worst kind of trouble, both legal and political."

"I need details, not half-assed racist assumptions. Was that all that the caller said?"

"No. He gave a gruesome description of what he'd done to the body. He spoke to the dispatcher for quite a long time. He even demanded that she repeat back to him what he'd said. When she did, he said he had one final remark. 'Tell Jake Dablo and Jimmy Song Bird to read the Bible verse that says vengeance is mine, sayeth the Lord. Tell them that the vengeance of the Lord has evened the count'. Then he hung up. The dispatcher immediately called the Chief of Police. He called me next."

Zeb removed a pen and notebook from his shirt pocket and wrote down the Bible verse.

"I drove up to Antelope Flats with Officer Tommy Horse Legs. We were the first ones at the scene. We were able to drive within thirty feet of the body. The killer had turned the remote location into an eerie sacrificial altar by placing candles around the body. They were still burning when we arrived."

"The only people I know who do rituals on Apache land are Apaches," said the sheriff.

"I recognized the girl right away as Amanda Song Bird, Jimmy Song Bird's granddaughter. And for your information, Sheriff, Apaches have more respect for the Medicine Man and his family than to ever murder any of them. Murder is a White man's disease."

Zeb tugged at the brim of his cowboy hat and shot a laser beam from his eyes to Eskadi's where they were met with dogged resistance. He reached across the table and grabbed the cassette recorder and forced the tip of his thumb down hard on the eject button. Slowly, methodically, he turned the small machine on its side and let the tape slide into his hand. He rotated it deftly between his fingers before dropping it into Black Robe's coffee. Eskadi's facial expression remained stoic, his eyes cold. Zeb signaled the café owner with a flick of the wrist. At his command, the leather faced café counterman limped over.

"My buddy here needs a new cup of joe. His attitude just did a swan dive into this one," said Zeb pointing to the cup.

"Cream and sugar?" asked the owner.

Eskadi cursed aloud in Apache. Having heard it before, the owner rolled his eyes.

"In that case, you'll have to take it as it comes," he said, returning to the counter.

"Enough of the bullshit, Black Robes. Let's cut to the chase," said Zeb. "You're here because the drunks and thieves you call lawmen don't know shit from shinola when it comes to a case like this. You need me to come in, solve your murder and save your political skin. But I'll go straight to hell before I become some sort of pawn in your hate the White man game."

"I didn't think you had the balls to step outside the White reservation," said Eskadi.

Zeb wanted to reach across the table and grab the Indian by the throat. His resistance to such an act was steeped in a long personal history.

"But because it's Song Bird's granddaughter, I'll help you out. Just remember it's not for you, and it never will be. If you try any more of your shenanigans, I'll split your head wide open and leave that big, college-educated ego of yours as buzzard bait."

Eskadi didn't flinch. Instead a small, wry smile appeared at the corners of his mouth.

"Are you done with your little tough guy rant, Sheriff? Look, whatever you think of me is irrelevant. Whoever killed the innocent child must have been evil incarnate. If he's White or if he's Indian, which I doubt, we still have to catch him. Let's focus on that."

"What else have you got?"

"She was slit open from here to here." Eskadi's gesture mimicked a knife entering the soft part of the belly just below the navel. He moved his hand slowly up his midline to his throat. "Then the killer reached inside her chest and cut out her heart. In the chest cavity where the heart had been, the killer placed an abalone shell. Song Bird's name was etched into the shell.

"Her heart? An etched abalone shell with the grandfather's name?" mumbled Zeb.

A horrible, sinking feeling weighed heavily as the unsolved murder of Angel Bright rose from the ashes anew. The stunned sheriff was wordless as he let the similarities of this case with that of Jake Dablo's granddaughter sink deep into his consciousness. The extreme lengths that someone must have gone to in order to end the life of an innocent child in such an exacting fashion chilled him to the marrow. This sort of ritualistic detail hinted at more than premeditation. It pointed toward an obsession.

"The body was taken by ambulance to the morgue up in Globe," said Eskadi. "The local coroner knew right away this murder was out of his league. He's called in a Dr. Louis Virant from Phoenix. He's a forensic expert in pediatric murder cases. He's driving down from Phoenix later today. It will probably be late tomorrow before we have a preliminary report."

"What did your people find at the scene?"

"Not enough. That's why I called you," replied Eskadi. "That's why we need your help. We've never seen this sort of murder before. I understand you have some experience in such matters."

Zeb Hanks' sterling reputation when it came to securing evidence at a crime scene had evidently crossed the reservation border. As a detective in the big city of Tucson the sheriff was driven to leave no stone unturned when it came to the minute details of a murder scene. His ego would have it no other way.

Creeping into Zeb's mind was the ugly thought that Eskadi was operating with some ulterior motive. Knowing the tribal chairman's politics, it wouldn't be at all surprising if he was protecting one of his own. Worse yet, he could be setting someone up for a nasty fall. The likelihood of deceit put a bilious taste in his mouth as he eyeballed Eskadi.

Zeb slapped three one dollar bills on the table and stood to leave.

"Anything else strike you as out of the ordinary?" he asked.

"Her hands were placed inside her body and the killer started to sew her shut." Eskadi looked pale as he continued. "Whoever killed her..." Eskadi slowed his speech as if he were groping for each word. "...dressed her in traditional Apache Sunrise ceremonial clothing. They situated her body with the head facing east and placed a lit candle in each of the four directions."

Eskadi Black Robes' words stopped Zeb dead in his tracks. Certain information about the mutilation and murder of Sheriff Jake Dablo's granddaughter, Angeline Rigella Bright, had never become public information. One of them was the fact that she had been found in clothing typical of the style used for the Mormon baptismal ceremony. Candles also had been placed around the body and were still burning when they found her. Angel Bright's heart, too, had been removed from her body cavity. Inside her halved torso was the *Book of Mormon* with Jake Dablo's name etched on the cover.

"Let's go have a look," said Zeb.

"Right."

5

T he two men walked to Eskadi's pick-up truck in stone-cold silence. The grinding of the gravel beneath Zeb's boots and the squeaking of the rusty restaurant sign seemed oddly amplified in the open lot. When Eskadi suggested they take his truck, a high riding four-wheel-drive vehicle, over the rough roads to Antelope Flats, Zeb reluctantly agreed.

Through the rock-hard, barren landscape, the men rode wordlessly as the hypnotic rhythm of traditional native drumming filled the cab of Eskadi's truck. The radio station, which brought the Apache Nation news and traditional music to the reservation, was one of the many innovations Eskadi had instituted as tribal chairman. As the men headed down the road, the music played softly in the background, pushing some of the anger from Zeb's head.

"How is Maya coping with this?"

"Understandably, she's in shock from losing a child. She has said very little since she found out."

"How about Song Bird?" asked Zeb. "How's he coping with the death of his granddaughter?"

"He's called in another medicine man to help out with a

prayer ceremony. Living in this moment of grave sorrow has hit him very hard. His spirit is weeping for his granddaughter and honoring his daughter's sorrow. Song Bird may be a medicine man and a wise grandfather, but he is also a man. Even those who provide for the spirituality of others go through crisis in times of doubt. I sense that Song Bird feels he has failed his community and his family."

Zeb was reminded of the weakness that the senseless death of an innocent child brings, even to the sagest of men. He also saw clearly how Eskadi's relationship with Song Bird could be helpful. Zeb knew eventually he would have to delve deeper into their camaraderie. Now was not the right time for that. It was enough at this point to know that Eskadi respected Song Bird. Eskadi's desire for resolution of the murder seemed to allow him to speak openly. But in the back of his mind, Zeb couldn't shake loose the idea that something more, something hidden, was motivating the tribal leader.

A rough and hardened dirt road flanked by alternating areas of stone-covered, rolling hills and flat desert spaces led them to where the body of Amanda Song Bird had been found. The wheezing, grind of the truck's engine as it climbed a steep incline and the sonorous tribal chant coming from the radio fusing with the sound of rubber tires slipping on smooth rock created additional discordance.

At the scene of the crime tribal police deputies exchanged nods with Eskadi. However, they avoided all eye contact with Sheriff Hanks. Eskadi led the sheriff to the spot where the girl's body had been found, pointing out bits of evidence he and the tribal officers had gathered. Eskadi then walked away perched on a boulder as the sheriff surveyed the scene. The tribal policemen, stone-faced and cross-armed in their crisp, federal uniforms, eyed every detail of his detective work with stern, unblinking stares.

Zeb crouched to the ground, resting on a single knee. As he surveyed the area just beyond the candle that had been placed to the north of the body, an unseen mockingbird serenaded the hideously brutal crime scene with a lush chorale of sweet desert voices. The eerily celestial soundtrack made Zeb's skin ripple with goose flesh.

In his shadow, where the child had been laid, a coagulated pool of blood, blackened from deoxygenation, lay atop the orangish-brown dirt. Staring at the death spot, his mind created the illusion of a slithering snake exiting its den. To his immediate left, a few sparse, intermittently placed drops of dried blood led toward the only open space in the immediate vicinity. A quick eyeballing told him it was a big enough area for a truck to turn around in without taking the risk of getting stuck in the sand or rocky ruts.

Zeb knew immediately the killing had been done where he knelt. Death had its way of leaving behind a faint echo. The homicide detective who had trained him taught him to believe the palpable resonance left behind at a murder scene was the fear and anxiety a dying soul experienced in their last living moments. Zeb, uncertain of the theory, knew from his personal encounters that the essence of murder didn't easily leave its place of origin. He could feel the absence of life chafing the surface of his skin. The taste of death danced on his taste buds as the acrid odor of dried blood and desert earth wafted through his nose and down his throat. Death presented itself with a feel, a smell, a taste, a sound.

Zeb slowed his thought process and stopped all internal thought. He focused on the natural world that surrounded him. He listened to the distant wind as it raced across the desert, interrupted only by the mountain. The child, Amanda Song Bird, must have screamed for help in her final minutes and cried out for mercy. The killer no doubt would have taunted her when he spoke. His planning would have made him confident and allowed him to relish the moment of total dominance. He probably was so brazen as to even let her scream her little lungs out. In this remote part of the reservation only the animals and the night air would be attentive to such shrieks.

The killer's presence oozed into Zeb's being. Instinct begged that he shake it off. But he didn't, he couldn't. This strange ability he had acquired, the sensing and imaging of the death of a human being, was a curse not a gift. He found himself becoming agitated as his neck began to pulsate and sweat.

"Who moved the body?"

Tommy Horse Legs meekly raised his hand.

"I helped the ambulance driver," he said.

"Show me exactly where she was laying."

"Right there," said Horse Legs. "In the middle of those candles."

"Show me," commanded Zeb. "Draw an outline of where the body was."

Horse Legs used his finger and traced the rough outline of a small body.

"It was about like that."

"About like that or exactly like that?" demanded Zeb.

"That's how it was," replied Horse Legs. "Wouldn't you say so, Eskadi?"

"Never, ever move a body without marking its location," barked Zeb. "Your stupid mistakes may make it impossible to find the killer. Do you understand that?"

Horse Legs retreated without responding.

Sheriff Hanks' eyes followed the trickling trail of blood back to the larger pool of sanguine fluid where the child's body had been ceremoniously displayed. His eyes followed the edge of the small box canyon and then back down the road. The makeshift altar was not visible from any vantage point. The killer had not chosen this spot randomly.

The embryonic stages of the hunt began in Zeb's mind by creating an image of what might have been. He visualized the killer and imagined his hands resting on the steering wheel, maneuvering his vehicle, probably an older model, into the small area where he parked. The man's hands would have been gloved. Fingerprints would likely be impossible to come by at the scene. The man, probably young, wouldn't have covered his face. There would have been no need. He knew he was going to kill the girl. Besides, if the message the killer relayed through the dispatcher to Song Bird and Jake was legitimate, the killing was personal. He would have wanted the girl to see his face. Her hands and feet would have been bound to immobilize her. Her mouth gagged to keep her quiet. That would require rope or tape which would leave marks on the body. The killer must have purchased it somewhere. When he did, someone would have seen him. That might be a good starting point.

A sickening question entered Zeb's mind as he envisioned the child lying on the ground. Had the killer raped his helpless victim? If the idiots passing as tribal police hadn't mucked up the scene, or better yet, called him before they moved the body, his trail of evidence would be wider and deeper. Zeb ground his heel into the dirt in disgust. Stepping back, he eyed the imprint his boot made in the sandy earth. The killer would have carried the child's body to his makeshift altar from the vehicle. He probably had her stuffed in the trunk. That meant footprints. Zeb walked the route from the candles to where he imagined the killer parked. There was no shortage of footprints. First glance told him that not one imprint in the dirt was singularly distinguishable from any other. The tribal police, all precisely dressed in the same standard-issue, military-style boots, had tromped all over the scene making a collective fundamental and irreversible mistake. They had destroyed solid evidence possibly allowing it to become little more than a ghost in the wind.

The real hunt inside Zeb's head was the pursuit of the killer's mistakes. The killer had been methodical but brutal, a combination of traits found inside the head of a smart but angry man. Maybe if the girl resisted, he had struck her knocking out a tooth. If she fought her attacker, there was always the chance that a piece of whatever she was bound with could have come loose and ended up on the ground. Maybe he would get lucky and find a paint chip from the killer's vehicle. He scoured the area on his hands and knees. Half an hour later Zeb had little more than skinned knees to show for his trouble.

Standing, he felt the heat of the Apaches' glare on his every move. He returned the unfriendly glower as he concentrated on the murder weapon. The scalpel used to eviscerate the young woman had to have been kept in a bag or a toolbox. Murderers, he knew from experience, have an obsessive, almost sexual relationship with their killing weapons. If he had to place a bet, the killer probably still possessed the weapon. He had also likely kept the extracted heart. The seed of hatred in Zeb's soul toward the murderer was quickly germinating.

Zeb paused, breathed deeply and forcefully reminded himself to leave his emotions out of the equation. Hating the killer and despising the shoddy work of the tribal police would do nothing to return life to the dead child. He turned once again to the sacrificial altar. A ghostly vision of an adult carrying a young person's body became crystal clear. The killer might have cradled her in his arms or carried her over a shoulder, gunnysack style. Such an action would leave traces of blood and hair on his clothing. They would have to be disposed of or cleaned. Find the clothes, find the murder weapon and find the killer.

Zeb's mind began to speed up as he considered what kind of relationship the killer developed in his mind with Amanda Song

Bird. He may have treated her like his prey or like a sick dog that had to be put down or, worse, much worse, a despised lover.

The sheriff shifted his gaze and viewed the landscape through a different set of eyes as he shifted from fantasy back to fact. Cholas and prickly pear cactus dominated the green vegetation. The undergrowth was typically sparse and brown. A small barrel cactus glistened gold, looking out of place as it jutted out of the soft rock on a south-facing side hill. A ground squirrel flitted across Zeb's field of vision a hundred feet away. No birds, save the mockingbird, were singing. When the mockingbird rested momentarily from its mimicry, the entire landscape seemed absent of life.

The hard, rutted road the killer drove in on was situated in a shallow ravine, between the rocky hills. It was recessed and lower than the surrounding area. The cold remoteness of the spot once again struck Zeb. In the direction of Bylas, the road quickly disappeared around an incline. A hundred yards in the opposite direction the road dead-ended. This was a spot of extreme isolation. It was a desolate place that only a loner would have an innate feeling for. It was the perfect spot for a murder.

The lack of any solid evidence paid homage to the cunning nature of the killer. This was a well-planned, well-thought out crime, likely even rehearsed. The sheriff's instincts told him he was dealing with an extraordinarily rare killer, a highly intelligent and highly motivated one. He jotted down a few notes and called to Eskadi who was still perched like a wild animal on the boulder.

"Eskadi," he demanded. "Have your men get me a good set of tire tracks from all their vehicles. I want a copy of yours too. Have them cordon off a perimeter a hundred yards extended out in each direction from the candles. They need to do a square inch by square inch detailed search of the area. Tell them to keep their eyes open for clothing, footprints, blood, gloves, a piece of tape, a band aid, chip of paint, strand of hair, anything that shouldn't be there. Think they can handle that without screwing it up?"

Eskadi passed the order to the lieutenant, and the men went to task.

"Have the tribal police keep an eye on the road leading up here. Ask them to call me with the license plate numbers of any cars or trucks that come up this way," said Zeb. "That means all Whites and all Indians. Instruct them not to stop anyone. Have them discreetly tail anyone who looks suspicious. Make damn sure they don't fuck up. They've done enough of that already."

The mockingbird cried out once more. This time an almost humanlike, high-pitched scream came shrilly through its beak. The Apache policemen stopped and turned in its direction.

Staying behind after the others had completed their work and gone, Eskadi and Zeb stood silently over the ground where the mutilated body of Amanda Song Bird had been found. An otherworldly sensation crept through Zeb's being. It was a brutish, ugly feeling that he tried to shake off, but he couldn't.

The men returned to the truck and headed down the hill toward Bylas, the radio humming lowly in the background.

"We have lost one of our children." The disembodied voice of the announcer carried with it a heavy tone of sadness and sorrow. "The dead body of Jimmy Song Bird's granddaughter, Amanda, was found today in Antelope Flats. The Graham County Sheriff's department is assisting tribal police in the investigation."

Haunting, spiritual chanting music resonated in the cab of the truck. Deep, baritone, Apache male voices blended in harmony with the alto-soprano wailing of the Apache women, whose intonations were contrasted by the constant din of a mellow, tranquilizing drumbeat.

Eskadi hummed softly, peacefully with the funereal chant as

puffs of pure white clouds drifted lazily in formation across the horizon.

"Who the hell called them? That's all I need, for the killer to have up to the minute information on what we're doing," snapped Zeb.

Eskadi stared ahead at the road as Zeb gave him a hard once over.

"If I'm going to work on this case, you're going to have to learn to keep your mouth shut," cautioned Zeb.

"I need your help, but you've got to remember the reservation is sovereign Apache land. It doesn't belong to the White man," said Eskadi. "My people need to know what's going on in their community."

Zeb pulled the brim of his hat down and stared out across the barren wasteland of the lower San Carlos. His thoughts turned to Maya Song Bird, the dead girl's mother. Since moving back to Safford from Tucson, he had thought many times about going out see her. He found himself regretting that he had not taken the time. In fact, he hadn't had any contact with her since the night he left town fifteen years earlier. That night, the night before he left for boot camp, he, Maya Song Bird, Jenny Dablo had celebrated at Red's Roadhouse. They got smashed on pitchers of beer and shots of tequila. Under the false euphoria of alcohol, they vowed eternal friendship to each other. Now, years later, both women had lost their daughters and Jenny Dablo Bright was dead.

When Jenny died, Zeb had gotten word from a friend of his in the Phoenix Police Department. The official cause of death was accidental vehicular homicide. She had fallen out of a car and was run over by a truck. The actual cause of death was acute alcohol intoxication. Her life, one that was already racing downhill on greasy skids, took a serious turn for the worse after her child, Angel Bright, was murdered. Zeb sat up straight and squared off his hat.

"Head south when you get to the highway," he said. "I want to take a little trip up toward Song Bird's place."

"I don't think that's the right the thing to do," said Eskadi. "We should at least wait until he and Maya are there."

"And let more evidence possibly get destroyed? You and your men have done a good enough job of that already. Besides, we need to have a look at the spot where she was allegedly snatched."

"What makes you so sure she was kidnapped up there?"

"I'd tell you why, but I'm afraid you'd want to call your reservation radio station and have them make a public announcement."

"I need to know. How do you know where she was taken from?"

"Horse Legs has a big mouth. He let it slip that Maya said her daughter was running between her house and Song Bird's just before they discovered her missing."

Zeb could see the information was news to the tribal chairman.

"He shouldn't be punished for accidentally saying something that might help me," said Zeb.

"He won't be," said Eskadi. "That's not the way Apaches operate."

Approaching Wildhorse Canyon, Zeb realized he had forgotten what a beautiful oasis Song Bird's land was amidst the harsh and barren reservation land. Returning to the stunning surroundings triggered a memory, an Apache yarn Song Bird had spun one long ago autumn morning when Jake quizzed Song Bird about how many generations of his family had lived on this piece of land.

"It was so long ago," said Song Bird, "that when Usen created the earth, he stopped by with a housewarming gift for my first grandparents." The serious look on Zeb's face had been met with a gleeful howl from Jimmy Song Bird.

As Eskadi parked his truck at the end of Song Bird's yard, Zeb thought of happier days and the dozens of times he and Jenny Dablo would pull into Song Bird's yard and honk for Maya. Back then Zeb had a beat up old truck that could barely make it up the road without bottoming out. His well-known boyhood crush on Maya didn't stop Jenny from coming on to him. As he looked back on it, maybe sleeping with Jenny when it was Maya that he truly cared for was the real reason he had left town. Jenny had slept with half the boys in the county and most of the men. Under the influence of alcohol, Zeb had given her his virginity behind the Roadhouse in the building the youngsters fondly called Red's Shed.

It wasn't long after their tryst that Jenny got pregnant. And when she married a greaseball trucker she met at Red's, she confided in Zeb that it wasn't the trucker's kid. She confessed to marrying him because he had money and she could get out of town fast. The real father of the baby, she said, would remain a secret locked in her heart. Though Zeb had slept with Jenny only once, pangs of guilt that Angel may have been his daughter loomed large.

Zeb got out of Eskadi's truck and headed immediately down a small arroyo to the home of the murdered child. The thicket of cottonwood and acacia trees formed a fortress-like canopy overhead, keeping the area cool even in the heat of the midday sun. Maya and children of the Song Bird clan for generations had played games in this peaceful spot where elders took siestas, children giggled happily and teenagers wooed one another.

Zeb listened to flower-hopping cactus wrens and purple finches chirp out greetings and warnings as the men encroached on their turf. If only they could talk, he thought. If only I could see through their eyes. A soft breeze sweeping through the canyon whistled through the cottonwoods as Zeb envisioned Song Bird instructing his granddaughter in some of the same lessons he had taught him.

Zeb scoured the area in search of the smallest of clues, seeking anything that would link the killer to the private world he had invaded. When he found nothing, Zeb felt his faith being tested. Doubts about his ability to solve the child's murder came creeping in. Overhead a mockingbird shrilled out in mimicry, 'ah-ha, ah-ha, ah-ha'.

"We should leave this place until Song Bird returns," said Eskadi.

"Let's wait here for a few more minutes," said Zeb.

"We should go," insisted Eskadi.

"No," said Zeb firmly. "Not yet."

Waiting for some mystical, magical happenstance to guide him, Zeb lay down on some soft grass in a shady spot and closed his eyes. For what seemed like the first time in his life, he heard nature not as individual sounds, but rather as a symphony. Nature's amalgam of lush music was interrupted by Eskadi's whining drone.

"Maya and Song Bird are in Globe with the body. We should respect the sanctity of their property until they can be here with us."

Zeb rose to his feet and made his way to the truck. A shiny object, glinting in the sunlight thirty or so feet down the road, caught his eye. He walked directly to it. Bending down he picked up a sliver of thin yellow-orange plastic. It looked like a broken section from a tail light cover. He slipped it into his shirt pocket.

By the time the men were on the road back, the sun, sinking into the western landscape, radiated a lavender hue atop the surrounding mountain peaks. The magic peacefulness of twilight time in the desert bled deeply into the day's disturbing emotions.

"Tomorrow we need to talk to Song Bird and Maya," said the sheriff.

"Much is happening with them right now," replied Eskadi. "Maybe you could give them another day or two?"

"No. The sooner I can talk to them, the more likely it is they'll be able to help us. My guess is they may know much more about the murder than they realize. The quicker I can ascertain what they actually know, the greater chance we'll have a suspect on the near horizon."

"According to Apache tradition, we shouldn't yet disturb the family."

"Tell Song Bird it's at my request," said Zeb. "Tell him for the sake of finding the killer and bringing him to justice that I said cultural beliefs needed to be put on the back burner for now."

The men parted, agreeing to meet early the next morning at the Silver Spur.

Zeb's heart felt hollow during the long drive back to Safford as he recalled the time and circumstances surrounding the murder of Angel Bright. He had only returned from Tucson and been back in town acting as Jake's deputy for several months when the murder happened. Even though he had seen many murder cases in Tucson and his experience was deeper and broader than Jake's in such matters, he didn't push back when the sheriff kept him at arm's length during the investigation. Now, under these circumstances, he found himself regretting his lack of aggression in that matter. At the time, Zeb assumed Jake suspected Angel could have been his child. It appeared to be some sort of grand gesture to save Zeb the pain and agony of dealing with the child who might have been his own flesh and blood. Zeb now realized just how flawed Jake's thinking was at the time. But Jake never saw clearly when it came to family.

For years Jenny had caused Jake nothing but heartache. The death of his granddaughter was the final crushing blow to a troubled relationship. Shortly before her death, Jenny, in a drunken rage, went so far as to publicly blame her father for failing to catch the killer of his only grandchild, her only child. Once the best lawman in Southeastern Arizona, practically every resident of Graham County had held him in the highest regard. In those days, when people talked of Sheriff Dablo, they had always used a tone of reverence. But the events of October 18, 1992 changed that forever.

Zeb bore no ill will against the former sheriff, nor thought poorly of him for the way he handled the investigation of his granddaughter's death. After all what man could go through what Jake Dablo had, finding his granddaughter, dead and gutted like a slaughterhouse animal, her tiny heart crudely ripped from her body, apparently while she was still living. What man could go through all that and remain sane? And what man would not succumb to the punishment from the hateful heart of his only child?

6

J ake Dablo, former Graham County sheriff, slowly
awoke to face the dread of another day. His eyelids,
sealed shut from encrusted sleep, concealed heavily
bloodshot eyes. The lonesome coo of a solitary dove,
nesting in the dilapidated gutter of his rusting trailer, called to
him. He weighed his options. Should he bother to open his eyes
or should he simply return to the escape that only sleep brought
him? He waited until the deep ache in his head gave him no
option.

A thin splay of early morning light crept through the
yellowed window shade, allowing only minimal light into his
bedroom. The tattered window veil was shut not so much to
keep out the daylight but rather to keep Jake from having a view
of the night sky, the enchanted sphere his grandfather had
taught him to love. The same night sky whose celestial formations revealed the myths of life and death. The heavens above,
home to the ancient Gods as well as his own God, had cast him
aside in his moment of need. His heart, seeded with grief, could
no more forgive his Maker and forget the pain of his loss than it

could cease to beat of its own volition. Ruefully, he opened his eyes.

Beads of foul, alcoholic sweat oozed from every pore of Jake's slowly decaying body. As the light of day filtered through one blurry bloodshot eye and then the other, he gazed at the water-stained ceiling tiles directly overhead, ceiling tiles that now, sadly, replaced the stars in the sky of his long-lost normal life.

The once robust and healthy cowboy sheriff coughed, clearing the phlegm from his blackened lungs. His chest tightened sharply as he rolled onto his side, reaching to the floor for his nearly empty pack of Marlboros. A second raspy hack ejected greasy sputum from his lungs, which he swallowed, barely noticing its mucous consistency and smoky taste. The scarred fingers of his bony hand fumbled across the linoleum floor until they grazed against an open matchbook. Pulling a single, limp cardboard stick from the book, he glanced at the cover. 'JoeBob's Bar—Good Eats and Drinks'. Stewart sandwiches nuked in a radar range and pickled eggs tasting of burnt rubber and reeking of sulfur were hardly good eats, even to a high mileage drunkard like himself. Jake managed a pathetic grin as he flamed the match head. The odor of burning sulfur stirred a wave of nausea where his gut met his throat, quelling his short- lived smile.

The first drag of tobacco seared his lungs and cleared the milky vision from his tired eyes. Cupping a hand behind his head and pulling the grimy covers halfway over his protruding gut, he blinked repeatedly, hoping to create a little moisture for his painful, reddened eyes. His arm drooping over the side of the bed held the growing cigarette ash nowhere near its intended receptacle. Eyes transfixed by the water stains overhead, Jake squinted his sunken brown eyes, hoping to rid himself of the illusion he envisioned. But it was not to be. The discoloration on his ceiling manifest itself as a small child, a young girl playing happily...smiling...normal...normal life...normal existence...a different time...one that no longer existed. The brown stains melted into gray, then black, as the image assumed the proportions of a dead child lying on a cold desert floor surrounded by burning candles, snakes slithering over her lifeless form. The murder of Angeline Bright had never been solved. The sad details of her life were as gut wrenching as the crime itself. Her mother's pregnancy had been stressful and plagued with drunkenness perhaps leading to a defect that caused the child to lisp. Little Angel was only eight years old and in preparation for her Mormon baptism when she was kidnapped and mercilessly slaughtered. A cold chill ran up and down Jake's spine as his memory allowed the imprisoned details of the funeral day to drift into his thoughts. Angel's frail body, dressed in white and lying in a child-sized casket, was the epitome of purity and innocence. Jake felt weak as details of that fateful day enveloped him. Angel's missing heart was never found. Because of the brutal nature of the murder and because it was never solved, the case had stayed in everyone's mind. Jake eventually resigned as sheriff and devoted his life to finding the killer. But his obsession with finding the murderer cost him more than his job and career. Gone also was his wife, Dawn, and their twenty-five-year marriage. But the ultimate price of his manic fixation was the lack of a firm footing in sanity based reality.

Jake inhaled deeply as a foggy memory of what now seemed like the distant past came floating through his mind. He had cracked under the strain. A little stint, courtesy of the state mental institution in Phoenix. Psychiatric talk therapy and sedative medications did little to quell the pain burning inside him, followed. With rest and solitude, Jake figured out what the doctors wanted to hear. When he found the stamina to play their game, the state ruled him sane. They released him back into society. Free from the institution but still held captive in his heart and mind, Jake moved into an abandoned desert trailer and began an existence amounting to little more than a steady diet of rot gut whiskey and barely edible food.

But his demons didn't stop easily. His daughter, Jenny, a hell raiser since her early blossoming puberty, was the town trollop before she could drive and the town drunk after her daughter was murdered. Too many nights at Red's Roadhouse had introduced her to a life of rough sex, cheap booze and mind-twisting drugs. When she died tragically a year after Angel's death, it took everything Jake had to barely maintain his already loose grip on the bottom rung of the ladder.

Before the psychiatrist, before the Rorschach testing and before the lithium, those images on his ceiling were severely disturbing to Jake. Now they had become merely a way of life. Jake closed his eyes, but the images remained, trapped in a space between muted reality and sublimated hallucination. The cigarette dropped from his hand, landing near the ashtray as he fell back asleep and into the only possibility of escape. But in his sleep were dreams, dreams that held the terror, the loss and the fear that permeated his very being. If there was a God in heaven, He had abandoned hope at the doorstep of Jake Dablo.

The big Dodge Dakota hummed down Highway 70, returning the sheriff to the Safford city limits shortly after sunset. The billboard above the Town Talk lured him in for a quick bite. It said, 'Better than Home Cooking (And We Do the Dishes!)', He had a few hours of pencil pushing and paper shuffling awaiting him at the office. That kind of crap could wait. It wasn't going anywhere. Supper and a little jawboning would go a long way towards lifting the burden of the day a few inches off his shoulders.

The lifeblood of the café was Doreen Nightingale, a Rubenesque woman in her middle thirties with ash-blonde hair stacked like a whirling beehive on her head. She was never without a smile on her face and an acerbic quip at the tip of her tongue. She wore lipstick which defined Ruby Red. Blush with sparkling flecks dotted her cheeks making her eyes twinkle electric blue. This unique packaging created a sassy, sexy, bohemian, free spirit that Zeb found attractive from the moment he had first laid eyes on her.

Doreen was new in town by Safford standards, a half dozen years. She had won her way into the hearts of the locals who treated her as one of their own, often confiding in her over a cup of coffee. She was privy to most of the wag and tongue gossip that kept the ears of Safford burning. Never one to betray a confidence, Doreen knew when to keep her mouth shut and when to spread the word. Casual and confidential conversations may well have brought people into the café, but it was one delectable Tex-Mex burger that kept them coming back. Sheriff Zeb Hanks had a distinct weakness for both.

"Evening, Sheriff," squeaked Maxine Miller.

The painfully shy waitress who doubled as the Town Talk's assistant manager was the polar opposite of the brassy Doreen. Zeb had once asked Doreen why she had come to hire such a mousy little gal like Maxine. Doreen told him she did it for the same reason she rimmed the chili bowl special with orange slices, that being no particular reason at all. It was just her way of doing things. In the same conversation, she suggested that if he didn't like the way she did things, she was certain any of the other cafes in Safford would be more than glad to have him dirty their dishes. Like just about everything surrounding Doreen convention took the back seat to invention.

"Howdy do, Sheriff Zeb." Doreen's voice echoed through the back half of the cafe. "How's everything hangin' tonight?"

The sheriff was eminently thankful that no one, other than the blushing Maxine, was within earshot of Doreen's wisecrack. The general public could easily make hay with a remark like that one, especially in a town as Mormon as Safford. Zeb's gut reaction was to respond in a sexually playful fashion to Doreen's quip. Some clever retort of his own. Low and loose and full of juice or looking for a spark and a place to park. But he thought better of it and let her sass linger in the air unrequited as he hung his ten-gallon hat and took a stool at the counter.

"Good evening, Miss Doreen. I'm a starving steer," replied

Zeb. "What you got cooked up special for a lonesome cowboy tonight?"

Doreen leaned forward, exposing more than a little of the creamy, white flesh of her generous bosom as she placed utensils and a paper place mat in front of her sheriff.

"Everything round my neck of the woods is special, hon," she said.

The sly wink accompanying her sexual innuendo produced a rosy pink tint on the sheriff's cheeks to say nothing of the stirring it created elsewhere. Standing nearby, a wide-eyed Maxine was all ears.

"Well, in that case, I would like..."

The sheriff paused, soaking in Doreen's coyish body language and flirtatious ways like rays of sunshine on a cloudy winter day. The look in her eyes, a subtle swaying motion of her hips and a full profile view of her tightly confined breasts made it clear her playful game was meant for his pleasure. This was exactly what he needed after a day like he had.

"I would like..."

The sheriff felt his heart firing at high speed, like the time he had that fancy coffee at a Starbucks in Phoenix. His mouth became suddenly dry, his tongue as chalky as that of an old hound dog waking from a long nap. If she wasn't having a little fun at his expense, she was coming on to him like gangbusters. For a man who could take one look at a criminal and know what they were thinking, Zeb was as illiterate as a newborn babe in the woods when it came to reading Doreen. His voice box cramped as it uttered in a stammer.

"I would like..."

"What you'd like...is me," whispered Doreen.

The sexy waitress's sultry voice sent Zeb into a near dream state as, once again, she flexed her femininity inches from his face. His eyes fought from crossing as, with a delicate touch, the scarlet nail of her index finger traversed the soft space between her breasts in ever so sensuous circles.

"What you'd like is me...to make the decision for you. Isn't that right, sunshine?"

The pink hue of the sheriff's cheeks deepened to crimson. Even his chest felt flush.

"Here you go, tiger."

Doreen reached beneath the counter by the cash register. From a secret space, she grabbed a Chinese fan, flared it open and refreshed the sheriff by creating a gust of cool breeze for his hot skin.

"You're actin' like a radiator with a busted fan belt and lookin' like a fresh beet just plopped into boilin' water. Maybe I'd better call in Doc Yackley to check your blood pressure?"

Handing the fan to the sheriff, Doreen performed an effortless pirouette and floated into the kitchen. The sheriff, transfixed by the gentle side to side swaying of her tightly garbed buttocks, gave the fan a genuine workout.

Witnessing the red-hot interchange, the sheepish Maxine dropped her jaw as well as a plate she was clearing from a table. The loud crash of ceramic on vinyl was little more than a faint background noise to the pair involved in the mating ritual.

Zeb was still fanning the blush from his face when Doreen returned from the kitchen with his dinner. He barely managed to lower his thermometer reading.

"One Wednesday night special. Made just for you with these here lovin' hands," said Doreen with a wink. "With a little somethin' extra special tossed in at no charge."

Her teasing hint of 'somethin' extra special' caused him to gulp as his imagination shifted into high gear at the thought of what that might mean.

"One Tex-Mex with all the trimmings, black beans with Momma's homemade salsa and one Braeburn apple, sugar, cut just the way you like it. Bite size with no bruises and no rough edges around the core."

If the roadway to a man's heart had a single route and that being through the stomach, Doreen should have been an executive for Rand McNally.

"This is perfect, just perfect. Thank you, Doreen," said Zeb. "How can I ever thank you for such good cooking and for looking after me the way you do?"

"You'll think of somethin', Sheriff," she said. "A man of your style and imagination can always think of somethin'."

As Doreen attended to some new customers, Zeb caught himself wondering how each bite could taste better than the last. Even more so he dreamed of how nice it would be to sit around and gab with Doreen until the moon was high in the sky. But duty called. He finished his fine supper and neatly tucked four crisp one-dollar bills under his coffee cup. Doreen, busy waiting on a customer across the room, rolled her head and tossed him a wink. He pinched the brim of his hat between thumb and finger and headed out the door. To feel better than he did at this moment would be impossible.

Sticking the pencil behind her ear, Doreen eyed Zeb's tight jeans as he left the café.

The Dodge Dakota practically drove itself back to the station as Zeb fantasized a thousand thoughts of Doreen. He daydreamed of lying in bed, half draped with sheets. Doreen Nightingale snuggled softly against his chest as he blew perfect rings of smoke out the open window toward a distant moon. But his castle in the air disappeared like the puff of smoke it was as he bumped against a stack of files Helen had placed on the edge of his desk, sending them flying in a dozen directions.

"What a freakin' moron," he mumbled to himself.

Hoping he hadn't undone too much of Helen's hard work, Zeb heard only the steady ticking of the grandfather clock as he picked up the fallen papers. A glance at the slowly moving clock hands set his mind in motion. Long ago he had trained himself to know what criminals were up to by the time of day. The hours between six and nine p.m. were his favorite because criminals generally socialized like normal human beings during these hours. It was a pretty safe bet little would happen until night passed into total darkness. He picked up the last of the files and mused.

"Let's see, what have we got here?"

Zeb blurted out an involuntary chuckle as he read the most recent complaint from the widow Grehlick regarding vandalism at the abandoned cotton mill. Deputy Steele's report stated the widow Grehlick was frightened by a snapping noise. When she stuck her head out the door to investigate, some youngster back talked her, calling her an 'old bitty'. The widow, well into her eighties, didn't take kindly to sass.

The sheriff recalled back when he and his older brother, Noah, had broken in their new slingshots on that very same building twenty-five years earlier. His old man had gotten a little liquored up that year and gone along to help bust out the windows. It was the only time Zeb ever recalled having fun with his father. Just about every boy who grew up in Safford over the past half century had tested his aim on that building. With forty or fifty vandalism complaints about the old mill during his tenure alone, the sheriff pondered how the building could possibly have any windows left unbroken. He set the widow's complaint to the side and gave the small stack of speeding tickets a quick once-over.

Four speeding citations, two issued for running a red light and one for an illegal U-turn by the deserted railroad tracks. The tickets, all issued to good taxpaying citizens, bore the signature of Deputy Steele. The sheriff knew she was anxious to prove herself, but there were better ways to make the right impression with the locals. He made himself a note to talk with her about the difference between the intent and the letter of the law. Jake Dablo had done the same thing for him after Zeb arrested the mayor for making an illegal U-turn. Passing a little practical wisdom and common sense on to her was part of the job.

Zeb straightened the papers and was about to push away from his desk when he noticed a telephone message taped to the shade of his desk lamp. The note, written in Helen's crispest handwriting, was straightforward and wholly unexpected. It said, 'Please Call Jake Dablo'. The sheriff flipped it over to see if Helen had written more on the back. She hadn't. He turned the note over and reread it. 'Please Call Jake Dablo'.

Zeb hadn't had a phone call from Jake in over a year, maybe more. A man like Jake Dablo was damn unlikely to wait that long between calls and not leave some sort of a message. However, it was October eighteenth, *the* black letter day in Jake's life. The lack of a message troubled Zeb as a brutally ugly thought came to mind. Could Jake be suicidal? Zeb knew that the down side of human nature often reached its nadir on anniversary dates of tragic events. The more the possibility of such an action seeped into his brain, the harder he worked to push it away.

"Nah, couldn't be," he assured himself. "Jake ain't like that. That's the coward's way out. Jake's no lily-livered quitter."

Zeb knew if Jake had been depressed, Helen would have heard it in his voice. Helen, just being Helen, would have passed that information along to him in half a heartbeat. Carefully peering over his secretary's desk, he garnered a quick look to see if perhaps there wasn't a longer message she had written but forgotten to put on his desk.

Zeb felt invasive touching anything in Helen's work zone. Carefully, he returned each item he moved on the immaculate desk to its original spot. As he returned a small box of paper clips to its original position, his hand brushed against a piece of scratch paper covered with Helen's doodling. Curious as to what filled Helen's mind when it wandered, he picked it up and held it under the light. She'd written the date, October 18, underlined three times with heavy lines. Following the 18 were three darkened question marks. Zeb lightly traced a finger across what she had written. October 18???

The sheriff stuffed the note to call Jake Dablo into his shirt pocket, nearly cutting his finger on the broken fragment of tail light plastic. Once again, his eyes were drawn toward Helen's absentminded musing. Rolling his fingers over the date, he reached into his pocket and reread the note before glancing up at the grandfather clock. It was getting late. Jake was probably three sheets to the wind, passed out in bed, hugging a whiskey bottle like it was some long-lost lover. Besides, if it really had been important, Helen would have done something to let him know.

Zeb walked back to his desk, wondering what Jake and Helen had discussed. Jake was a man of few words. Helen probably did most of the talking. He considered calling Helen. It was nine-thirty. She would be at the church for the Wednesday night Relief Society meeting until ten. With Helen at the helm, no elderly Mormon in the area went without comfort in time of need. Every sick person was visited daily, and no child's basic needs were left unmet. It probably wasn't a good idea to bother her when she was at her highest and mightiest. He winced, knowing he wouldn't sleep until he knew what was going on with Jake.

Trepidation caused his heart to flutter as he thought of the peacemaker that Jake had never drawn. Would its first use be against its owner? Jake had suffered enough for a dozen people in this lifetime. He didn't deserve to end it all by putting a slug from a revolver into his brain. If Jake did something foolish and Zeb had the chance to stop it and didn't, he would never forgive himself.

Zeb picked up the phone and punched in the numbers. If Jake didn't answer, it didn't necessarily mean he had killed himself. Twenty rings and no answer didn't settle the matter in his head or his heart. Sheriff Hanks took a deep breath, the fatigue from a long day making every bone in his body ache for a little shuteye.

"Goddamn it, Jake. Pick up the phone. Come on, Jake. Please pick up."

Listening to ten more unanswered rings did little more than give him a sore ear.

"Shit! Jake, you'd better be passed out drunk with a smile on your face if I'm driving all the way out there tonight."

8

The night sky, glistening in starlight, lit his way down the country back road to Jake's trailer. Zeb rolled down the window and listened to the night. Howling dingoes sang in the distance as a lost lamb bleated for its mother. The ewe's response was quick in coming, starting a call and response between the lost and the frightened. The desert, unforgiving and harsh, rarely made allowances for the weak and defenseless. Maybe the frightened baby sheep would be the exception rather than the rule.

Zeb felt a rush of relief when he eyed Jake's beat-up pickup parked with the keys in the ignition. But his spirits dampened when Jake didn't answer his knock.

"Jake? You in there?"

Through the mesh screen, Zeb's flashlight scattered beams into the living room. Nothing looked out of place but he found the circumstances odd enough to warrant letting himself in.

"Jake? It's Zeb Hanks. You asleep in there? Don't mean to scare you if you are."

Zeb made a quick scan of the room. No Jake Dablo to be seen. Nothing out of the ordinary, save the fact that maybe the trailer looked like it had recently been straightened up. Zeb found that unusual, but hardly a felony. Jake Dablo was fifty-five years old. He didn't need a baby sitter or a mother. Zeb continued his examination of the trailer.

On the wall over a small desk were letters of commendation and awards Jake had received over the years. Zeb eyed the coveted Arizona County Sheriff of the Year plaque and remembered how moved Jake was to be honored by his fellow lawmen. Next to the awards was a series of photos from happier times, pictures of Jake, his ex-wife, his daughter and his granddaughter. Days gone by, thought Zeb, days when people wore smiles more easily than they do today. On the desk was a photo that made Zeb's head spin in a double take. He looked closely at a series of pictures from his and Jenny's senior year, most of them from the senior prom. The largest photo was of one of three steadfast friends, Jenny, Maya and Zeb. Zeb shook his head. He looked ridiculously silly in long, curly hair and a skinny little mustache. Jenny and Maya both radiated the innocence and beauty that rides high on the faces of carefree youth. If he could only go back to that day knowing what he knew now. Though impossible, it didn't stop him from wishing it so.

Zeb exited the trailer and headed home. His fatigue was rapidly turning to exhaustion. He allowed himself to believe that Jake was fine to overrule a nagging fear that he might not be.

Plopping his head on his pillow, he considered the chance that the events surrounding October eighteenth were making him a bit paranoid. Giving himself a goodnight lecture on the absolute need for logic in a lawman's mind, he drifted off into a well-deserved and desperately needed sleep. But his slumber was short-lived when an all too real nightmare shocked him from his sleep.

Gasping and swallowing air under laborious breath, Zeb bolted upright in bed. A thick layer of sweat covered his head, dripping into his eyes. The dampness made his head feel clammy even though his face burned like fire. His pajamas were drenched and clung to his heaving chest. As Zeb struggled to catch his breath, his nightmare vividly replayed itself. Recounting the ghoulish nightmare, the sheriff wiped his forehead with a dampened bed sheet.

The macabre vision had a most peculiar setting, his imagined future wedding night. Zeb's bride, a stunningly beautiful Doreen Nightingale, her back turned to him, laughed as she began to remove her wedding dress for a night of impending nuptial bliss. The chemical reaction in his dream body as he watched Doreen undress bordered on a previously unrealized euphoria.

"Shave those rough whiskers for me, would you, pumpkin?" she asked as Zeb floated into the dream bathroom.

"I'll be right back, honey. My face will be as smooth as a baby's bottom."

Lathering his face with a cool, minty, shaving gel, his body shivered with anticipation. His warm hand, soft from lather, rubbed against a face that, in the mirror, beheld the happiest man wandering through dreamland. Each stroke of the straight razor gently removed nubbins of whiskers. His dream face was silky. Suddenly, his state of ecstasy was shattered by a blood-curdling scream. The razor slipped in his hand, slicing his face near the corner of his eye. Large drops of bright, red blood drained down his cheek into the sink where it speckled the white shaving gel. But the only pain he felt was the intense fear stinging every fiber of his being as Doreen cried out. His body tensed with every ounce of its strength as he attempted to move. But his effort was worse than futile. He was frozen, unable to act. Not a single muscle in his body responded to his brain's command to move. Her terrified screaming, ringing off the tiled bathroom walls, ceased as it melded into a guttural, muffled utterance.

He ordered his feet to march, but they reacted as though some unyielding magnetic force had immobilized them. His mind screamed her name, but no sound fell upon his ears. Gasping for air, he finally broke free from the gripping paralysis. He charged the bathroom door with the power of a hundred men, only to be soundly repelled. He heaved his shoulder against it a dozen times. Finally, with Herculean effort, he broke the door loose from its hinges. Once again, he found himself unable to move. This time he was frozen by the sight of Doreen's body. Lying on their wedding bed, naked, Doreen was freshly gutted from her navel to her neck. His eyes took in a dizzying display of exposed internal body organs covered with warm, sticky blood. But it was the sight of Doreen's still beating heart, lying on her breast, that buckled his knees out from beneath him. Kneeling over the body, his dreaming became suddenly lucid as his mind flashed between Doreen and the image of Amanda Song Bird's sacrificial altar in Antelope Flats.

Zeb shuddered as he pushed the nightmare from his head. Drenched in sweat and trembling with anxiety, he stumbled out of bed, groping his way to the bathroom sink. Splashing cold water on his hot face did little to calm him. He ran his fingers through his sweat-dampened hair, exhaled heavily and gave himself a long, hard stare in the mirror. Cautiously touching his face to assure himself of his own existence, he switched on the small light attached to the side of the mirror but quickly turned it off, not wanting to see too deeply into his own reflection.

Alert and alive but caught in a netherworld state of mind, he found his way back into his bedroom. Pulling open the top bureau drawer, he rifled through his socks and underwear in a vain search for cigarettes. His mind argued strongly that he had hidden some there months earlier when he was in the midst of cheating on the quitting process. As he became calmer, he remembered that he actually discarded the old coffin nails.

Still restless from his dream, Zeb walked barefoot through the darkened house to the living room. His little toe brushing hard against the leg of a chair returned his senses to near normal. In the silent darkness, he replayed the evil and frightening nightmare over and over. Detail after detail streamed through his consciousness, imprinting their latent images into his memory. Doreen's dress, pure white, her shoes, satin purple, the blood on his face in the mirror, orange and red, her heart, paling as it lay on her dying body, its beat rhythmically synchronous to his own inhalations.

His mesmerized state of mind was abruptly shifted by the raspy growl of a car's worn muffler. Zeb instinctively looked through the street-facing window. A light fog rested close to the street, a sign of rare, low-hanging moisture in the late desert evening. Edging back the curtains, he squinted out at the street, eyeing an old car limping down the road. One of the tail lights, which identified the car as a Ford, was broken. From the way the rear end hugged closer to the curb than the front, Zeb assumed it had a bent frame. He looked closer at the unfamiliar red car as it turned a corner under a streetlight. He tried to read the license plate, but the car was too far away. His mind, still awash with the lingering effects of the dream, flashed to something Jake told him on his first day of work many years earlier.

"Once you put on this badge, you've got yourself a twenty-four hour a day job. A policeman may sleep, but his mind never rests. Because of your dedication to the job of citizen safety, there will be times when you are the only hope for justice."

The racing rhythm that had overtaken Zeb's heart slowed to a more normal pace as he continued staring out the living room window. He blinked a few times and shook his head, hoping to shake the bad dream loose and push it a little further away.

Closing the curtain to ensure total darkness, Zeb headed to the refrigerator and poured himself a tall glass of ice-cold chocolate milk. He pulled a chair to the kitchen table and recounted the gory details of his dream one more time like it was some sort of crime he should solve, not merely a series of fleeting images he had no control over.

Wandering back to his bed, Zeb lay down on his back. He stared mindlessly at an intricately woven spider web in a corner where the wall met the ceiling. Slowly, the angst associated with the images of his nightmare oozed further into the recesses of his memory.

At six a.m. when the clock radio on the stand beside his bed began to sing, Zeb's eyes opened to see the spider's web had nabbed an unwary night critter. The local country and western station greeted him with a familiar refrain by Buck Owens, one of Zeb's favorites.

"I've got a tiger by the tail it's plain to see,
I won't be much when you get through with me.
I'm a losin' weight and a turnin' mighty pale
and it looks like I've got a tiger by the tail."

9

With one hand gripped tightly on the steering wheel, the killer took the corner a little too fast. The Coleman cooler slid across the leather seat, stopping when it jammed against the gearshift. The top popped open and dense dry ice fumes drifted upward. He inhaled deeply, carrying the aroma through his sinuses and deeply into his lungs. Wind sucking through the open window blew the thick air aside, revealing two small freezer bags. Each was filled with a single brownish, fist-sized object. He reached into the cooler and smiled as he fondled the frozen packages.

Driving down the dimly lit street, the killer eyed the big Dodge truck parked in front of the sheriff's house. He tapped his brakes lightly and slowed to a crawl as he checked to see if the lawman was awake. He knew that the sheriff's routine would be his undoing. It rarely varied. The lawman was always up early and at the office no later than seven-thirty. He knew the sheriff did some business and then took a break to visit that dolled up whore who ran the Town Talk. He made city rounds, visited the bitch again at the Town Talk and spent the afternoon back at the office or out making rounds. Most days he worked a little late.

The sheriff was so mundane that it required little or no thought to outline his every move. The killer laughed at the one-dimensional nature of the sheriff. Such a simpleton would never catch him. This little cat and mouse game was like a duel, one that would ultimately leave the sheriff dead on the field of honor.

Tonight the killer was calm, collected and cocky. He considered upping the ante. Maybe it was the right time to stick another bee under the sheriff's big ten-gallon bonnet. Maybe tonight he would add to his collection.

He turned again and headed toward the county jail. A couple of young girls drove by and waved, laughing. Were they laughing at him? Angry, he turned around and followed them as they headed north on the highway toward his turf, the lonesome and empty desert. He followed their taillights until they pulled into a ranch house. The loud music told him a party was going on. He pulled off the road, turned off his lights and sat, listening and watching. It was easy. Oh, so easy. His body tingled with excitement as he fantasized new victims. No one would ever catch him. His father's lessons had been too well learned to fall prey to mere mortals.

Pounding jets of scalding water beat down on Zeb's neck and back. He focused on the day that lay ahead as the lingering odor from the night's sweat-filled dream disappeared down the drain.

Stepping out of the shower and into a robe, he rubbed his head vigorously with a towel and checked on the time. It was six-thirteen, too early to call Jake. He wiped the fog from the bathroom mirror and began to lather his face. The sound of the furnace kicking on grabbed his ear. The cool morning temperatures of mid-fall signaled the possibility of an early arriving winter. The forced warm air escaping the bathroom duct struck the cool gel on his face, creating small air bubbles in the lather.

Lifting the razor to his face stirred the fading ghost of the previous night's dream. Zeb looked into the sink basin at the fallen drips of white lather, half expecting to see blood. With a second glance into the mirror he gave himself a scolding pep talk.

"Shake it off. It doesn't mean a thing. It was just a dream. Get a grip, bud. It's going to be a busy day. You're going to have to be sharp."

Most of the situations he would be dealing with today would be completely out of his control. For starters, he would be working on the enigmatic concept of *Apache time*. He found himself annoyed by the very notion of it. His father had mentioned more than once that many Indians seemingly glommed onto this unmeasured reference to reality as a convenient excuse to be lazy and shiftless. Maybe his old man was right about that. Zeb was worldly enough to know that disliking an individual Indian was a completely different story than painting the entire Apache Nation with the same brush.

Wiping the last dabs of shaving cream from his face, he considered what customs and rituals regarding the young girl's body would have to be followed in accordance with Apache tradition. Song Bird had probably contacted Geronimo Star in the Night to handle the spiritual and religious matters. Zeb reminded himself of the immense importance in showing respect to those beliefs. Under the circumstances, Song Bird may or may not appreciate Zeb's presence. At this point, there was no telling how that would play itself out. In light of losing his granddaughter, the wise Medicine Man's view of appropriate justice could be highly skewed. Being a man of much worldly experience, Song Bird probably had a passionate sense of justice. But being an Apache, he might see the necessity for stronger and swifter retribution. Such beliefs might preclude involving the Graham County Sheriff's Department.

Zeb's heart ached the hardest when he thought of Maya. After so many years, to finally have contact with her at such a terrible time in her life and under these conditions felt so wrong. Her heart would be broken. Zeb would undoubtedly provoke old memories. He should try and be there for her, but it was unlikely he would be much comfort at a time like this. Even less likely she would be looking for it from him.

Zeb tucked his shirt into his jeans. Slipping into his boots, the sheriff glanced up at the clock on the dresser. Six twenty-six. He grabbed his hat and placed it on his head and checked himself in the mirror. Before walking out the door, he instinctively grabbed the phone. What the hell, why not call? Why should he care if Jake was hung over or not? Jake was the one who had called him, not the other way around. Besides, Jake would understand a call from the sheriff doesn't necessarily come at a convenient time. It was better to find out right now what was on Jake's mind than to spend the day wondering.

When Jake answered on the first ring, he sounded alert, chipper, nothing like a man nursing a hangover. Zeb was almost lost for words.

"Hello," answered Jake, "and top of the morning.'"

"Jake, Zeb here. Best of the day back atcha'. You're up and at 'em mighty early."

"I was sneaking a peek at the pre-dawn stars and, let me tell you, they looked beautiful. Zeb, have you ever watched the gentle way that night sneaks away from the oncoming day? It's a real work of art. God bless the Creator and his wonderful ways."

"Uh, no. I can't say that it's something I've noticed. I'm sure it's beautiful."

"Well, have a gander sometime and let me know what you think. I'd be interested in your opinion."

"The next time I rise and shine an hour or so before daybreak, I'll sneak a peek."

"I can guaran-damn-tee you that you won't be any worse for the wear."

Jake's newfound attitude was as refreshing as it was unexpected. It was also quite inappropriate under the circumstances.

"Zeb, a couple of nights ago when I was staring up at the stars, a thought about you passed through my mind. Remember the night we were staking out those cattle rustlers just beyond the western base of Mount Graham, down there along the Snake River?"

"Sure thing. It was the first week I was back in town as your deputy. We nailed the bastards."

"We sure did. I was yammering on about the star formations and the stories they told. You were telling me about some bizarre murder case over in Tucson."

"I remember," said Zeb. "The Flickstein case."

"Do you remember anything I taught you that night about the stars? I bet you don't. But that doesn't matter because last night I remembered something about your murderer over in Tucson. You said what made him hard to find was that he hid in plain sight, right under everyone's nose. He was so blatantly obvious that you looked right past him as a suspect. Right?"

"That's right," said Zeb. "The killer was even a close friend of the family. They'd known him for years. Even after he confessed and gave up the location of the body, they couldn't believe it was him."

"But when they did finally believe it, didn't they exact revenge by burning his house down?"

"Nothing was ever proven."

"How much of an effort did you put into finding out if they had?" asked Jake.

"Not much of one," replied Zeb. "I was working homicide, not arson."

"When I was thinking about that case, it got me to wondering. Did you ever think the killer of Amanda Song Bird might be right here, in our own backyard? Sort of rubbing our noses in it?"

Zeb paused. In the background at Jake's house, strains of classical music, not the usual twang of country and western, drifted in the air.

"It's just a theory," said Jake. "Just a thought that came to mind. But think about it. By the way, thanks for getting back to me so quickly, I appreciate it."

"It's all right, Jake. I didn't get your message until last night. I tried getting a hold of you but you must have been out. During the day I was out of town."

"I figured you were up in Antelope Flats."

The grapevine had wasted no time in getting to Jake. News travels like contained lightning in a small town. But it could only have been Helen who told him about the trip up to the Flats. Zeb found himself wishing he had instructed her to keep it quiet to all outside parties, including ex-sheriffs.

"I know what you're thinking. You're wrong. Helen didn't say a word," said Jake. "Apache Jim gave me a call."

It was like the good old days when Jake was two steps ahead of the game. But even so, he suspected Jake was b.s.'ing. There was an almost one hundred percent chance that the old sheriff had Helen singing louder than the Mormon Tabernacle Choir at Christmas season. If he had also talked with Apache Jim, Jake had likely learned the history and timing of the kidnapping, the shape the body was in and exactly where it was found.

"I take it you know all about what's happened up in the Flats?"

"I know a little, but not all I'd like to," said Jake. "I was calling to find out what you've got. I sort of figured a sharp guy like you would have the jump on this thing already, maybe even have a few suspects in mind. Would you mind sharing what you know with a trusted ex-boss?"

His direct and firm manner sounded like Jake, the old lawman, not Jake the depressed, mentally unstable drunk. However, given the potential intertwined history of his grand-daughter's case with this one, Zeb hesitated.

"Zeb? What do you say? You're not going to stonewall me, are you?"

Zeb was uncertain of Jake's motive. His desire could be pure in heart by trying to help his old friend, Jimmy Song Bird or, as Jake called him, Apache Jim. Or it could be selfish. His intent could be to reopen the door to the investigation into the seven-year-old murder case of his granddaughter. Zeb's concern was that Jake's long-standing need to solve his granddaughter's case might make a grand mess of this one. There was also the remote possibility that redemption had sneaked out from whatever rock it had been hiding under for the last three quarters of a decade, and Jake could be of real help.

"You don't owe it to me, Zeb, and I would respect any decision you made."

"You're going to sniff around regardless of what I give you, aren't you, Jake?"

"Any help I can lend won't cost you a dime. I know how tight a sheriff's budget can be," said Jake.

"Let me ask you one question, Jake."

"Go ahead. I got my listening ears on."

"How are you? I mean, how are you really?"

Jake snorted a laugh through his nose that sounded like a muffled seal bark.

"By God, now there's a good question, and one I don't mind answering. I feel sort of like Rip Van Winkle. It's as though I've been asleep for years. I've got to tell you, for the first time since I can remember my heart is filled with hope and not the dread of despair. Zeb, I've been drowning my sorrow and pain in the bottom of a whiskey barrel for so long that I didn't know if I was sinking or swimming. But now something has happened. I got a glimpse at what is really eatin' at my craw, and it wasn't pretty. Lord knows, if I don't change right now, I might never get better. Believe me, I know it for a fact."

"I don't mean to be a skeptic, Jake. But are you sure you're up to the task?"

"Zeb, listen to me. Did you ever dream you was dead?"

"No," said Zeb. "Haven't had that one...yet"

"Well, I have, and believe you me, it's a nightmare you had better wake up from. It sort of breathes a little fresh air into your perspective on life. My existence has been a nightmare for two thousand five hundred days. That's right. Two thousand five hundred. You can count it up yourself. I put a pencil to it. Now I'm awake. Seven years in hell was enough. I've paid my dues. Zeb, I can help you, and I know you can use my help."

It wasn't Jake's words as much as how he said it that washed away Zeb's doubt and helped him make an instant decision.

"You're right. I can use your help, Jake. But if you get involved, you're going to have to keep me informed of every move you make. You make one move without my okay and your assistance will no longer be needed."

"Yours is the voice of authority, Sheriff. I'll let you know everything I do. Cross my heart."

"Then you're on the team. Here's what I have so far. Yesterday I went up to Antelope Flats with Eskadi Black Robes," began Zeb.

Even as Eskadi's name came rolling off his tongue, Zeb wished he had left the tribal leader out of the picture, at least for the time being.

"Is that rascal still on the war path against the evil White power structure?" asked Jake.

"You know the routine. White man bad. U.S. government dishonest. Apache good. Indian noble and honest. And Eskadi, him shit don't stink," replied Zeb.

Jake's resonating howl was the first belly laugh Zeb had heard from his mentor in longer than he cared to remember.

"A snake don't change its skin, a leopard don't change its spots," said Jake. "It don't make it wrong and it don't make it right. It's just the way the world works. No need to fret about it.

And no need to let it get in the way of you doin' your business. The law is, was and always will be the law. Now, go on."

"Eskadi called me at the office and asked me to meet him up at the Silver Spur."

"Does the old cowpoke that runs the place still stick his dirty fingers into the coffee cup when he brings it over?"

"I don't think the old fart has ever washed his hands," replied Zeb.

"Like I said, some things never change."

"And I'll bet Eskadi didn't reach for the check either."

"You got that right."

"Bein' that it was Apache Jim's granddaughter, did Eskadi at least back off a little with his bullshit?"

"Not so much."

"The little prick," said Jake.

"From there the both of us went out to the Flats. We drove out to the spot where Amanda's body was found, and I gave it the once over. Afterward we went over to Jimmy Song Bird's place in Wildhorse Canyon," explained Zeb.

Their conversation flowed so easily that in many ways it seemed almost like old times back when it was Sheriff Jake Dablo, the decision-maker, and Deputy Zeb Hanks, the detail man, protecting the county.

"Her body was found off Apache Route Double B. It's one of those winding, up-hill, dead-end back roads that crimps off into a small box canyon. There's one way in, one way out and nothing for miles around. I'd say it's the perfect spot for a murder."

"What did you find at the scene?"

Zeb paused, unsure of how many of the details about Amanda Song Bird's mutilated body Song Bird had passed on to Jake. The potential implications to Jake's mental health when he heard the grisly details could be devastating. They might even unloose the same demons that had pulled the rug out from beneath his feet years earlier when he ended up doing his stint at the mental hospital.

Jake's intuition was tuned in with the reasoning behind Zeb's hesitation.

"I know about the mutilation," he said. "Apache Jim gave me all the details. And I know you're concerned that since it was a child that was killed and mutilated, it may make me think of Angel. I respect your level of concern, but you can come clean with me. I can take it."

"It wasn't that I, uh..."

"Don't yank my chain, Zeb. It took seven long, crazy years, but I've come to grips with Angel's death."

"I believe you, Jake."

"And in my years as sheriff I've seen as much death in those canyons as blooming flowers. Hell, I've even seen a flower blooming right up through a dead carcass. Now that I'm okay, nothing is going to shock me. I've come to grips with all that. Now let's talk about the information you've got."

"All right. There were five candles placed around the body, one at each of the four directions and one above the head."

"Damn unlikely that was accidental."

"That's my thinking too. My original suspicion was that there may be some sort of Apache symbolism involved. I don't know exactly what signal somebody might have been trying to send. If the killer did have something symbolic in mind, like some sort of religious ritual, you couldn't help but wonder if our killer isn't from the reservation," said Zeb.

"When the time is right, we should go over that possibility with Apache Jim. I'd be damn interested in hearing what he's got to say about the set up with the candles at the crime scene. The time and the place could be significant too. It might even be that some freak is practicing a little bit of black magic."

"It looks that way on the surface."

"What do you think the odds are that the powers that be out on the reservation might be covering for one of their own?" asked Jake.

"That's a distinct possibility. In fact, when I met with Eskadi before we went to the scene, he tried to tape record everything I said."

"He's a sneaky little imp. Keep a close eye on him. I don't think he can be trusted," said Jake. "By the way, you didn't let him record you, did you?"

"Hell no. He's lucky he didn't end up eating the tape with one of his donuts."

Jake's laugh was more a snarl than a giggle.

"His men mucked up the area," continued Zeb. "They treated the area more like a picnic ground than a crime scene."

"Could be a ruse," suggested Jake. "One of the tribal police might be involved somehow. That would make the possibility of getting any real evidence from the tribe damn near impossible. You'll never get one cop to snitch on another, no matter what the situation."

"The thought crossed my mind. There's one other thing, too. The dispatcher who took the call from the killer said the caller sounded like a young white male."

"What did you expect? You think the Apaches are going to point the finger back at themselves?"

"Not hardly."

"I guess the real question is, who do you trust?" asked Jake.

"Myself," replied the sheriff. "I trust myself."

"Good. Never let go of that. When you start doubting your own actions, there is hell to pay," said Jake. "Say, by any chance the killer wasn't generous enough to leave behind any key piece of evidence, was he? Tire tracks? A piece of clothing? Blood samples?"

"Not a single decent footprint. Like I said, too many ill-trained reservation police tarnished the area. We got some decent tire casts, but I'll be damn surprised if that isn't a dead end. There was a lot of blood at the scene."

"You think the blood samples are going to give you anything?"

The memory of musty blood mixed with fine desert dirt forced its way into Zeb's mind.

"We've got plenty of fluid to work with. The greatest quantity was taken from a single large pool the body was lying in. It's a long shot, but I'm hoping we can find the killer's blood from some single drops away from where the body was lying. We sent samples to the regional lab in Phoenix."

"Any blood under the fingernails? Broken fingernails? Signs of a struggle?"

"I haven't seen the body yet. Goddamn Eskadi and his men hauled it off long before they called me. He did say both hands were covered in blood. It appears from what they said that the blood on the hands was entirely the girl's. The truth is Eskadi and the tribal policemen have no more idea than the man in the moon how to evaluate a crime scene. I'll never know exactly how much good evidence was destroyed."

"Were the hands stuffed into the open body cavity?" asked Jake.

Zeb hesitated. It was a point he had planned on avoiding.

"And was there an attempt to sew the body cavity shut?"

"Yes, on both accounts," replied Zeb.

Seven years in the bottom of a whiskey barrel, Jake was still as blunt and direct as ever, even when it came to the intricate and horrible details that made this crime so similar to the one that had ended his career.

"What aren't you telling me, Zeb?" asked Jake. "I get the feeling there's something else you want to say."

"Well, there is something else, but it's nothing that I can really explain. When I was at the scene, standing back a distance, I was suddenly overcome with ...this is going to sound crazy."

"Murder is crazy, Zeb. You sensed something, didn't you?"

"I'm not much of one to believe in ghosts and that sort of thing, but I was certain the spirit of the dead girl was trying to reach out to me, speak to me. I tried to shake it off, but my emotions seemed to get the better of me. That makes me sound like some sort of a nut, doesn't it?"

"That sort of thing isn't crazy, Zeb. Dead people leave all sorts of traces behind. Things you and I will never fully comprehend," said Jake. "Pay attention when that happens. You never know what will be revealed. You've got to always trust your instinct in circumstances like that."

"I rely on facts, Jake. My intuition can point me in a direction, but only facts can make a case. That's something I learned in Tucson a long time ago."

"Zeb, remember that out there in the wild it's a different world than in the big city. You kill someone in the desert and what lingers behind doesn't fade away quite as quickly as it does when the murder scene is surrounded by people and traffic and noise and bright lights."

"Yes, sir," said Zeb. "I'll keep that in the back of my mind."

"Did you order a search of the surrounding area?" asked Jake.

"Yes, but we didn't find a thing."

"How'd you leave the crime scene?"

"We cordoned off the area. If you're going to go up there, you should be aware that I had Eskadi order the tribal police to keep an eye on anyone traveling up and down the road. I advised them not to interact with anyone they saw, but to tail them, get license plate numbers and call me ASAP. I have no idea if they're disciplined enough to follow my orders, and I wouldn't want you getting shot at."

"I can take care of myself."

"I didn't get a strong feeling the killer would return to the crime scene."

"I'd guess you're right on that account. It's far too easy to be spotted in a remote area like that. I'm certain the killer, if he's as clever as he appears to be, would recognize that."

"I'm sure you're right about that. I still think it's good procedure to keep a close eye on the location for at least a month, just in case."

"If it's one of their own and the tribal police know who it is, that won't do us a damn bit of good. And, if they know who it is and want a little taste of revenge, we may end up with nothing. Or, worse, one Apache corpse rotting somewhere in a very large and very remote section of the reservation."

"That's hardly the kind of justice I'm hoping for."

"Others might disagree with you," said Jake. "Frontier justice, both on and off the reservation, has a long history in Graham County."

Funny words, thought Zeb, coming from a man who made a career out of following the letter of the law.

"After that we drove out to Apache Jim's place," continued Zeb.

"His daughter lives in that small adobe just down the hill, right?"

"That's correct. At the scene, one of the deputies let it slip that Song Bird is fairly certain his granddaughter was abducted on a trail that joins the two houses. I walked along the path and did a brief search of the area."

"Find anything?"

"Nothing to speak of except a broken piece of a tail light on the road. I suppose that could have come from his truck or

Maya's car. I'll look into it. But as far as anything that would indicate a struggle or a forced abduction—nothing. I'm planning on heading back out there and have another go round once we've talked with the family."

"Make certain you respect Apache Jim and Maya's wishes. I know you want to get all the information as soon as possible, but I also know from personal experience the pain Song Bird is going through. Don't press him. Cut him a little slack. The emotions surrounding the death and autopsy of a child are a living nightmare. When he's ready, he'll give you everything he knows."

Zeb couldn't help but notice this was the first time Jake had called his friend Song Bird instead of Apache Jim.

"Yes, sir. Song Bird's up in Globe with his daughter and the little girl's body as we speak. I'm headed to Bylas right now to meet up with Eskadi. Then we're headed to Globe. I'm planning to talk with the coroner. I was also planning on chatting with Song Bird and Maya. I'll see how things go once I get there."

"Zeb," said Jake, "I would really appreciate a phone call from you when you get back."

"Of course, Jake. You will be the first to know."

11

Eskadi was standing next to his truck, facing the warm rays of the morning sunshine and sipping coffee. He seemed lost in thought and totally ignored Sheriff Hanks' truck as it drove into the parking lot of the Silver Spur. Pulling past the tribal leader, the sheriff got out of his car and walked into the Silver Spur. A few moments later he walked out with a steaming cup of coffee in his hand.

"You're late," said Eskadi.

"I'm running on Apache time," snapped Zeb. "Let's go."

Passing over the dry bed of Ranch Creek, just outside of Cutter, Eskadi started to explain to the sheriff what approach he was going to take with Song Bird and Maya.

"The Athabascan, my people, have nothing in our tradition that relates to an autopsy. My opinion is that the entire process is a desecration of the spirit. An autopsy goes against our fundamental belief system and can only be considered an impure act. Slicing up a dead body is the White man's way of doing things, not the Apache's."

"What if it helps us find the killer?"

"And what if it doesn't?" asked Eskadi.

"If your men hadn't traipsed all over the crime scene, we might have been able to get along without this. But being that I can't bring back evidence that has been destroyed, and I don't want to bury evidence along with the body, I don't have any choice in the matter."

"It goes against sacred tradition and defies the wishes of the Great Spirit. Personally, my opposition to autopsies will never change."

"And I'm opposed to sloppy police work. That's never going to change either."

Eskadi rubbed his eyebrows and sighed.

"But, unfortunately, Song Bird feels differently than I do. He said he changed his mind about the need for an autopsy after talking to Jake Dablo. To be honest, I was shocked. For a man of his stature and dignity to go against tradition is unheard of. But as a Medicine Man, his wisdom is far greater than mine, and I will not directly question his actions."

Zeb knew Eskadi was blowing hot air. The tribal chairman had no real say in the matter of the girl's autopsy. It didn't take an expert in Apache culture to know that Song Bird's wishes, as Medicine Man and tribal Elder, superseded those of Eskadi.

"Song Bird understands what must be done to find justice," said Zeb. "His experience in the world is much greater than yours."

The men crossed the Globe city limits in stony silence. The old mining town, built on a series of washes, had experienced a recent revitalization with the reopening of the mines. When Zeb noted most of the downtown buildings were occupied with new businesses, many of them Indian artist galleries and Native American tourist shops, his comments were met with a mild grunt.

A sign on Main Street directed them to the hospital. The magnificent structure, built courtesy of a legislative copper tax initiative, sat on a crested hilltop high above the rest of the city, next to the executive mining offices.

At the front desk, a receptionist pointed a solitary finger toward the morgue. Tucked away in the distant corner of the basement, a pair of well-worn aluminum doors were topped by a sign that read simply, 'Morgue.'

Zeb's boots echoing on the Saltillo tile floors in the gloomy, poorly-lit corridor represented the only sign of life. Bending forward at the waist to prevent his hat from scraping against the low ceiling, Zeb's nostrils were filled by the septic odor of cleansing chemicals.

Just outside the metal doors was an arched entryway leading to a small waiting room. Inside, Song Bird, Maya and Geronimo Star in the Night, the Medicine Man Song Bird had called on, sat in the corner chanting lowly. None of the three acknowledged Eskadi or Sheriff Hanks as they entered the room.

Sheriff Hanks stood hat in hand, respectfully quiet, looking toward the floor. Eventually he raised his eyes and fixed his gaze on Maya. The long flowing hair falling around her face failed to hide the pain emanating from her soul. A heavy sadness overcame him as he noticed a slight quiver on the lips of his old friend.

Eskadi took a seat opposite the other Apaches. Eyes closed, he joined in the mourning song. When the chant ended, Song Bird gave a traditional Apache greeting.

"Hon Dah."

Geronimo Star in the Night reacted only with his eyes as he handed Eskadi a piece of sage drawn from a bundle sitting between the four of them. Eskadi accepted it with a reverent bow. Maya, the saddened mother, blinked twice as if coming out of a trance and then bowed her head forward, acknowledging no one. Zeb felt removed from the circle as he watched empathy radiate between the kinsmen whom all carried an equal burden of death in their eyes.

"Hon Dah."

Song Bird's voice, weakened from circumstance, extended an arm to greet Eskadi.

"May the Great Spirit welcome your daughter to her grand-mothers and grandfathers," offered Eskadi.

Song Bird and Geronimo Star in the Night responded to Eskadi's benediction with a hauntingly beautiful death hymn. Eskadi joined them. Maya, head tilted forward, rocked back and forth, silent tears falling from her face.

Sheriff Hanks was immersed in the vision of his childhood friend as the chant of the Medicine Men carried him out of his body and returned him to the death scene. Awash in this strange, new sensation, the rhythm of his beating heart spoke, not with sadness nor sympathy, but rather in a complex array of previously unheard inner voices. His body felt feather light, almost invisible. The brim of his hat vibrated in his fingertips. The uncanny, harmonious blend of love and loss created a sense of extraordinary peace deep in his soul. The sheriff's sense of time and awareness of reality faded into nothingness as he entered a hypnotic-like trance. His unconscious spoke to his subconscious mind and demanded that it too seek out the heart of the killer.

"Zeb."

The whispering voice was accompanied by a sharp rap on Zeb's shoulder. His unfocused eyes fluttered. Slowly his atten-tion began to return to the world around him. Several seconds later he realized he was still in the morgue's small waiting area.

"Come on, come with me," said Eskadi. "The coroner is waiting for us."

Irked at being jilted away from his peaceful state of altered awareness, Zeb followed the tribal chairman down the corridor. The sound of Eskadi's soft doeskin leggings contrasting with the thumping of his own cowboy boots helped drag the sheriff further out of his fog. The crack of Eskadi's knuckles on the coroner's office door returned the sheriff to his normal state of consciousness.

"Come in, come in. You must be Sheriff Hanks and Eskadi Black Robes. I'm Dr. Bruley and this is Dr. Louis Virant."

The men exchanged handshakes, and the boisterous Dr. Bruley pointed out chairs for the men.

"Dr. Virant, an old classmate of mine from the Arizona Medical College, is a nationally recognized expert in the field of pediatric forensics. That's why I called him in."

Louis Virant, a tall, slim and neatly coifed middle-aged man whose roughhewn hands belied the surgical nature of his work, winced as he worked Cornhuskers lotion into his digits one at a time. Dr. Finnian Bruley, an elfin-like character whose uncombed head of shocking red hair stuck straight up, looked more like a seafaring ship's doctor from a bygone era than the desert doctor he was.

Dr. Virant sat behind a large metal desk in a squeaking chair. He fiddled with a tape recorder and fussed with three tapes, each marked ASB, Amanda Song Bird.

"I'm going to tape record our autopsy findings," began Doctor Virant. "I will use these tapes to assist me when I fill out the final official documents. These tapes and the required state forms will become part of the official, legal record. If you have any questions during the process, let me know and I will stop the tape."

The distinguished coroner peered over the top of his bifocals at the lawmen.

"Any questions, gentlemen, before we begin?"

Eskadi and the sheriff shook their heads in unison.

Dr. Bruley pulled a pipe from the inside pocket of his jacket, tapped it against the palm of his hand and added some tobacco from a pouch lithely pulled from another jacket pocket. Seemingly lost in his own world, Bruley began quietly poking at the tobacco as his cohort inserted a cassette tape and pressed the record button. Still playing with his pipe, Dr. Bruley spoke.

"This is autopsy number nine-nine-zero-one-six. The body is that of an approximately thirteen-year-old female Native American of the San Carlos Apache tribe. Legal name of the deceased is Amanda Song Bird. The date of birth, as stated by the deceased's mother, is June twenty-second, nineteen eighty-six. No official state or tribal birth certificate available. The date of death is October eighteenth, nineteen ninety-nine. The time of death approximately two a.m. Dr. Finnian Bruley is the attending physician. The special autopsy physician and physician of record is Dr. Louis Virant. This autopsy is being performed by and for the State of Arizona and in accordance with current statutes and regulations."

Dr. Bruley paused to light his pipe. He continued.

"The body of the deceased was brought to the St. Mary's Hospital in Globe, Arizona by unnamed officials of the San Carlos Reservation at zero six hundred hours on October eighteenth, nineteen ninety-nine. The body was ornately clothed in what was described to me by a family member as a traditional Apache Sunrise ceremonial dress. The mother and grandfather of the deceased have provided all requested information. That data is attached to the document file and is marked exhibit number one. There are no prior medical records. The mother states her daughter has received no traditional medical care. The official results of the autopsy of Amanda Song Bird will be given by Dr. Louis Virant of Phoenix General Hospital, Phoenix, Arizona."

Dr. Bruley reached forward, stopped the tape recorder and turned a serious face to Eskadi and Zeb.

"Gentlemen, parts of the autopsy report will be very graphic. If you become ill, there is a bathroom two doors down the hall and to the left."

Dr. Virant began with a litany of mostly indecipherable medical terms regarding the relative health of the component systems of the young girl's body. Had it not been an autopsy report he was dictating, anyone listening to the glowing remarks about the excellent condition of the young woman's body would have assumed they were dealing with a healthy human being rather than a corpse... until he began to describe the wounds.

"A large incision, appearing to have been made by a highly sharpened instrument of surgical quality, begins near the midline, approximately two inches inferior to the umbilicus and extends cephalward to the tip of the xiphoid process. A second opening, transverse in nature and perpendicular to the first incision, was made approximately one inch superior to the umbilicus. That cut extends from the anterior head of the tenth rib on the right to the anterior head of the ninth rib on the left. The heart and surrounding tissues were grossly removed from the chest cavity via the opening made by these incisions. The chest cavity as presented is absent the heart. The aorta, superior vena cava, inferior vena cava and all pulmonary arteries appear to have been cut with a compressive, shearing force, indicative of a scissors like instrument."

Dr. Virant paused and sternly gazed at the two lawmen before proceeding with his report.

"Based on the abrasions on the spleen and pancreas, as well as the pooling of the blood in the chest cavity, it is my opinion the patient was alive when the injuries were sustained. The preliminary blood work has shown no evidence of anesthesia or narcotic analgesia. It is my opinion that the young woman would have been aware of what was happening to her until lapsing into pain-induced unconsciousness. The chest cavity was crudely resewn with broad stitches using nylon fishing line."

The thought of removing the heart of a living child and the terror she must have felt during this most heinous of acts was almost too much for Eskadi to bear. His dark Apache skin turned ashen gray. The pungent odor of formaldehyde wafted into the small office as hospital attendants wheeled a gurney through the morgue doors.

"No sperm was found in the vaginal canal or in the uterine cavity. However, there were numerous cuts and incisions on the labium. The hymen remains intact. I find no evidence of rape or sexual molestation."

Dr. Virant flipped off the recorder. Twiddling his thumbs methodically, the doctor appeared to be detailing in his mind the report he had just dictated. After a moment, he turned the recorder on for an addendum.

"The oral transcription of this report was witnessed by Dr. Finnian Bruley, attending physician, Eskadi Black Robes, Chairman of the San Carlos Apache tribe, and Zebulon Hanks, Graham County Sheriff. It is currently fourteen thirty hours."

Dr. Virant stopped the recorder and addressed the men curtly.

"I will have my report transcribed immediately. When it is completed, I will send a copy to the hospital front desk for you. It should be ready within two hours. Would you like to have a look at the body?"

"No," said Eskadi. "Absolutely not."

"Yes," said Zeb. "Please."

The malodorous, acrid aroma of heavy chemicals blasted Zeb's senses as he followed the doctors into the examination room. Inside, Amanda Song Bird's body lay on a cold steel table covered to the neck by only a thin hospital sheet.

"We've already closed her up," said Dr. Virant.

Zeb stared at the body. Amanda Song Bird's outward appearance was that of an innocent sleeping child. The horror that must have ruled the last minutes of her life was nowhere to be seen on her face.

Dr. Virant pulled the sheet to the child's waist, exposing where she had been mutilated. The precision with which the doctors had closed her wounds neared perfection.

"What's that?" said Zeb, pointing to the corners of her mouth.

"Glue from the backing of duct tape. It covered most of her mouth. The killer left the right quarter of her mouth uncovered. There was also some glue on her teeth. We cleaned it up."

Zeb reached under the sheet and lifted the dead girl's hand.

"We've cleaned them up. They were covered with blood. The men who brought the body in said that they were partially stuffed into the open body cavity when they found her. They likely fell out when they moved the body to bring it here," said Dr. Virant. "We're having the blood from beneath her fingernails matched for type against her own blood. It will be a miracle if we find a second blood type there. We found nothing about her hands that would indicate any major struggle. If you look at the wrists, you'll see bruising and discoloration."

The doctor held them up for the sheriff to see.

"He must have bound her wrists with rope while she was alive. In her attempt to free herself, she abraded the surface of the skin. There was no rope binding her when she arrived here."

"Did the people that brought her in say whether she was bound or not when they found her?" asked Zeb.

"They indicated that she was not bound when they found her."

Zeb placed the small hand back on the table. Dr. Bruley recovered the child's corpse and lit his pipe.

"Do you perform many autopsies on mutilated murder victims?" asked Zeb

"Sadly, more of them all the time," replied Dr. Virant.

Sheriff Hanks glanced in his rearview mirror as he signaled his exit off Highway 70 onto County Road 6. A left turn would take him directly to Jake's. A right turn led to the only entrance to Hells Hole Canyon, home of the fabled Apache burial ground as well as a half-dozen ancient rattlesnake hibernation dens. The coarse, grinding sound of compressed gravel under his truck's tires was a welcome change from the monotonous hum of paved road.

Heading east onto the poorly maintained tertiary road, he eyed a small whirlwind of dust and sand rising on an early evening breeze creating a dust devil. As it scooted across the desert floor, a singularly vivid recollection from his youth came to Zeb. It was the week of the fourth of July in the bicentennial year. An American flag hung proudly from every streetlight on Main Street in Safford. Zeb pedaled his bicycle to the Western Wear General Trading Store. After buying some baseball cards, he took a seat on an old wooden bench outside the store. He was engrossed in reading the player's statistics and chewing gum when an old Apache called Big Bear, who looked to be about a hundred years old and claimed to be a descendant of the great Chiricahua Apache warrior, Cochise, tapped young Zeb on the shoulder.

"Come over and sit next to me," commanded Big Bear. "I'm going to tell a story that every Indian boy has to understand before he becomes a man."

The progeny of the feared warrior Cochise with golden eagle feathers in his hair and a string of bear paws around his neck was a local legend. When he told a story, even the men who hated Indians listened in awe. This day he had a tale just for the eager ears of one young man.

"The clever coyote plays pranks on the wise as well as the fool," he told Zeb. "And the dust devil is one of his most clever and very best tricks."

"Why?" asked the wide-eyed innocent.

"Because the dust devil has the power to fetch away the possessions of people who have too many things. The dust devil has the ability to pick up objects and move them around. It might carry them to another rich man's house, or it might drop them at the doorstep of the poorest of men."

"Why would he do that?" asked young Zeb.

"If you listen instead of chattering like a baby squirrel, you might find out," admonished Big Bear. "If you are given something by the power of the dust devil, it is your choice what to do with it. You can keep it, or you can return it to its original owner. The intent of the yellow-eyed coyote is much more than just creating a dust devil to carry something from one place to another. Any big wind blowing down from the mountains and across the desert could play such an easy trick. The coyote is smarter because he also attaches spirit to the object. If the coyote trickster brings you a gift by way of the dust devil and that thing was obtained dishonestly, you receive the bad luck attached to an ill-gotten gain. But, on the other hand, if the object is a gift from the Great Spirit, it is now yours to have freely and enjoy completely. That, young man, is the trickery of the sly coyote."

Not five minutes after hearing the story, a five-dollar bill landed at young Zeb's feet courtesy of a dust devil. Immediately racing to the five and ten-cent store, he squandered the entire five bucks on penny candy, eating until his stomach was about to burst. Now, twenty-five years later, Zeb rubbed his stomach, recalling the pain of the three-day-long stomachache that followed. But the story stuck like so much hardened glue in his memory for a second reason. Big Bear had gently placed his craggy, weathered hand on top of Zeb's head just when Zeb was wondering, how can you possibly tell what sort of fortune is attached to something that arrives on the wind? The old Apache had laughed as he pulled his hand away from Zeb's flattop haircut. Looking directly into Zeb's youthful eyes, he told him, "the problem is, young man, it takes a wise man to hold an object in his hands and know it's fate and fortune. It is something most men can never know. It is something most men never even think of."

Zeb was absolutely certain Big Bear had the power to read his mind by simply touching the crown of his head. But when he asked his dad to corroborate the newfound belief, his old man scoffed at him and gave him a whipping for listening to the ramblings of a 'drunken old Injun'.

Dusk sneaked across Jake's property line in concert with Zeb's truck. The change of light created what seemed to be an illusion. Mysteriously absent from Jake's yard were piles of empty booze bottles, bundles of yellowed newspapers and the discarded heap of rubble left behind by a messy, chronic inebriate. Replacing the debris was a sitting area complete with a picnic table, chairs and an umbrella large enough to provide shade for a small group of people. At the end of the trailer on a small pad of freshly laid cement was a mounted telescope pointing toward the heavens.

But the most shocking sight for the sheriff's eyes was Jake Dablo sitting at the picnic table. Dressed in crisply pressed khaki pants and shirt, clean-shaven and looking hale and able bodied, Jake appeared to have shed a decade off his aging face. Zeb did an involuntary double take. The clarity and serenity in the old sheriff's eyes was something that had been missing since the death of Angel Bright.

"Zeb," Jake shouted, "by God, but it's good to see you. I was sort of expecting you'd be showing up about this time."

Jake reached out and shook Zeb's hand, nearly crushing his fingers in the process.

"Good to see you too, Jake. Looks like you cleaned the place up a little."

"This rat trap was just like me, a stinking, rotting mess. You know how it goes, garbage in, garbage out. But you should also know all messes, including personal ones, can be cleaned up."

Jake rip snorted a laugh. Letting go of the vice grip he had clamped on Zeb's hand, he took a step back and sized up his former deputy. Zeb found himself standing a little straighter, as though Jake were still his boss and giving him a military style inspection, just like he had when he first came to work for him.

"Yes, sir, young man. I can see the job of Graham County sheriff agrees with you. But an old timer like me can also see that it's wearing you down just a bit too," said Jake, slapping Zeb squarely on the back. "Take a load off. We've got some serious ground to cover."

Zeb took off his hat and set it on the table. Jake grabbed the cowboy hat by the crown and placed it on his own head.

"You still wearing this old thing?" Jake asked. "I'd have thought by now it wouldn't hardly have any shape left in it. I figured that Doreen, that wild filly of yours, would have up and made you spring for a new one."

The thought of changing hats never entered Zeb's mind.

"You know where that hat came from?"

"Of course I do. You gave it to me when I was about thirteen," said Zeb. "Hell, I can still remember the day."

"No, no, no," Jake roared. "Before that. Did I ever tell you where I got it?"

"No, as a matter of fact, you didn't."

"I should have 'cause it's got a little bit of a story attached to it."

Zeb gently flicked away some dust that had settled on its well-worn brim.

"Song Bird gave that ten-gallon contraption to me about fifteen years before I gave it to you," said Jake. "He won it in an all reservations championship bow and arrow shooting contest. He nudged out a couple of Navajo boys from up by Chinle."

"I didn't know that."

"Even though Song Bird won it fair and square, he never once placed it on his head."

"Why not?" asked Zeb. "It's a fine-looking hat."

"Old Song Bird was a bit of a radical himself back in those days, not unlike Eskadi Black Robes. He claimed it would be bad luck for him if he ever wore it. You see, Apache Medicine Men in those days wouldn't wear cowboy hats. Back then, well, it was taboo, sort of what it would be like if an American soldier wore a Nazi uniform. At that time, Apache Medicine Men would only wear Indian headdresses."

"Is that true?"

"Hell, I don't know for sure. That Song Bird can be pretty

quick to pull your leg and spin a yarn when he figures he can pull a fast one over on ya'. For all I know, he stole the damn thing."

The wind kicked up unexpectedly, pulling a single piece of paper from the stack Jake had laid on the picnic table. Zeb instinctively reached for it as it flew by at shoulder level. He nabbed it cleanly without putting as much as a crinkle in the paper.

"I see your hands are as good as they were back when you were the leading receiver for the conference champion Safford Tigers in '83."

Zeb chuckled.

"That was a long time ago."

As Zeb spoke, his eyes homed in on the headline on the sheet of paper the dust devil delivered to his hands.

Autopsy Report:
CURRENT DATE: October 19, 1992
NAME: Angeline Rigella Bright
DATE OF DEATH: October 18, 1992

The sheriff made eye contact with Jake as he handed him the paper.

"Have a sit down, Zeb," beckoned the former sheriff.

Zeb hadn't heard Jake use that particular expression in years. It was the phrase Jake used whenever he was about to 'go to school' on somebody. The last time Zeb heard the former sheriff talk this way was way back, way back when Jake used to smile freely, before the death of his granddaughter.

The last time Jake went to school on Zeb he was carrying on about how the legal system let some of the real criminal element slip through their hands like so much sand through an hour-glass. Jake raved for most of a day about how justice, real justice, was not available for the common man. Rich people, he ranted, could buy justice in the courts, whereas regular folks too often got the shit end of the stick. Zeb also remembered that Jake had ended his lecture by warning him that regardless of how justice was served, it had to follow the letter of the law. Now, tonight, the long-suffering Jake Dablo had the corners of his mouth upturned again.

Zeb took a seat as the setting sun cast a long shadow across the front of the trailer. The multi-armed saguaro standing sentinel over Jake's property was party to a family of baby cactus wrens who bobbed their skinny necks and gaped their open mouths in wait of their mother's return. Just above the distant horizon a sliver of a moon was rising to greet the night.

"How was the trip up to Globe?"

Zeb withdrew the neatly folded coroner's report from his back pocket and handed it to Jake.

"Here, see for yourself."

Jake paused momentarily, fingering the report as he examined the official coroner's seal before setting the document on the table. Reaching into a shirt pocket, he removed a set of wire-rimmed glasses. He toyed with the bifocals as he waited for his eyes to focus. Zeb watched the emotional metamorphosis as blood rushed to Jake's wrinkled face, smoothing his skin and further turning back the hands of time. From a rounded slump, his posture became upright and erect as Jake slowly devoured each word of the report he held in his weathered hands. Studying the body language of the man who had taught him so much, Zeb observed the pain of deep-seated sorrow in the facial demeanor of his one-time mentor. Jake removed his glasses, reached into his pocket and pulled out a bandanna that doubled as his handkerchief. Pausing to wipe clean his glasses and dab the corners of his mouth, Jake neglected to wipe away a tiny tear that clung to the corner of his eyelid, leaving it to evaporate in the dry desert air.

"Let's go inside," Jake ordered.

Zeb followed a few paces behind the former sheriff. Once inside, Jake marched directly to a file cabinet large enough to cover the entire corner of the small living room. Opening the top drawer, he grabbed a file thick enough to cover the spread of his gnarly fingers. The label of the tattered file read ANGELINE RIGELLA BRIGHT. Jake's familiarity with the file became evident as he reached into the middle of hundreds of sheets of paper and pulled out what looked like an invitation. He placed it gently on the table in front of his guest.

"Here."

Jake stood over Zeb, arms stuck deep into his pockets. He said nothing as the sheriff slowly reached for the envelope. The upper, right-hand corner of the envelope was stamped and post-marked. The cancellation date was clearly legible, Oct 9, 1992. Zeb carefully withdrew the contents. Inside was an invitation addressed in a child's scrawled handwriting.

Grandma Dawn and Grandpa Jake Dablo
238 North Fifth Street
City

F rom the childlike handwriting, Zeb assumed Angeline Bright must have addressed the letter. The date on the envelope was only days before her death. He removed the inner envelope and opened it. As Zeb suspected, it was the official announcement of Angel's baptism. He set the invitation on the table in front of him, leaving it open.

"Look at this," said Jake.

Calmly sliding the autopsy report in front of Zeb, Jake tapped a finger on the third paragraph.

"Read *this* line," Jake said firmly. "Read it out loud."

He tapped down heavily with his finger again.

"The child's body was dressed in clothing typical of that worn during a Mormon baptismal ceremony," read Zeb.

"And note the date," demanded Jake.

"October 18, 1992."

The words had barely escaped Zeb's lips when Jake thrust a second piece of paper in front of him.

"Now look at this."

With the swipe of an arthritic finger, Jake pointed to a specific line in Amanda Song Bird's autopsy report. Zeb read the simple sentence aloud.

"The body of the young woman was clothed in traditional Apache Sunrise Ceremonial dress."

"And this."

Jake pointed to the official date of death, October 18, 1999.

"Same day."

"And one other thing." Jake's lips quivered angrily as he read aloud from Angel's autopsy report. "The hands of the victim were placed into the open wound, fingers interlocked, as if in prayer."

Jake had it all laid out in black and white.

"Both children were preparing for an important religious ceremonial rite. My granddaughter for baptism into the Mormon Church and Apache Jim's granddaughter for the Sunrise Ceremony of the Apache Tribe."

Zeb nodded, rubbing his temple.

"Killed on the same date, October the eighteenth. Murdered in the same ritualistic style, gutted like lambs at the slaughter, hearts removed from the bodies and replaced with religious symbols. The hands of both the girls were placed inside their bodies. The physical environment of the crimes is identical, remote and isolated. The five burning candles placed at the four directions and above the head, identical."

Jake's words, an expressed mixture of long-awaited relief compounded by fear, burned hot on the sheriff's ears.

"Zeb, I know for a fact that the same goddamn son of a bitch committed both murders."

The sheriff knew he was in for another sleepless night.

13

Helen Nazelrod sat at her desk just outside of the sheriff's private office. She looked up as her boss briskly whisked past. His face carried the look of grim determination. His boot heels, striking down hard against the wooden plank flooring, sounded mean and angry.

"Helen, could you get a hold of Eskadi Black Robes for me as soon as possible. Tell him I need to speak with him now. And that means the sooner the better. I'll drive out to meet him if that works for him. Tell him I can leave right now. When you have him on the line, ask him if he's talked to Song Bird today. No wait, I'll ask him that myself."

The machine gun way he was firing off orders was the antithesis of his usual interaction with the secretary.

"Sheriff, why don't you sit down for a minute. Let me get you a nice cup of coffee and I'll ring up Mr. Black Robes," said Helen.

The soothing tone of Helen's voice made the sheriff realize just how rapidly he had been firing off orders. A deep breath later he felt his heart palpitating heavily. His mind couldn't shake the macabre image of the sliced open chests of Amanda Song Bird and Angel Bright, their little hearts pumping away, gripped by the killer's hand and yanked from their innocent bodies. The sorrow in his ghoulish image made him lightheaded and anxious. The sheriff's muscles tightened almost to the point of snapping as he felt the weight of the responsibility for closure of the heinous deed bearing down squarely on his shoulders.

"That would be fine," he said. "Just do it now."

Sitting down, Zeb began loudly rolling his fingertips against the desktop. The rhythmic tapping of his fingers on the wood served to calm him. His head began to clear. With a concerned look, Helen placed a cup of steaming brew in front of her agitated boss.

"Here you go. Black coffee, fresh pot," she said.

"Helen," he said.

"Yes, Sheriff."

"Thank you."

"Of course, Sheriff. Now let me see if I can round up Mr. Black Robes for you."

For the thousandth time since he had been elected sheriff, Zeb realized Helen was the grounding force he counted on in times like these. He had barely swallowed his first sip of hot java when Helen reentered his office.

"That was fast," said the sheriff. "Did you get a hold of him already?"

"No, I didn't. But I've got Mister Jimmy Song Bird standing by my desk," replied Helen. "He says you want to see him."

"I do," said Zeb. "Bring him right in."

Helen escorted the Apache Medicine Man into the sheriff's office and departed, making certain to leave the door slightly ajar.

"Sheriff," said Song Bird. "Jake called me last night after you left his place. He told me you wanted to talk to me."

"Thanks for stopping by. I know this is a tough time."

"Jake told me those closest to the victim often know much

more than they realize. I'm here to help you. I'm here to help find justice for my granddaughter. Her spirit must have rest."

"I appreciate that, Song Bird. We are all seeking the same thing."

"Do you have any idea who might have done this?"

"I've been searching my mind ever since it happened. I really don't know anyone who could do such a thing."

"Horse Legs tells me you think your granddaughter was taken from the arroyo between your house and Maya's."

"Yes."

Song Bird proceeded to give the sheriff a detailed, minute by minute account of his granddaughter's last hours on earth. She had been snatched without a sound or any sort of warning in broad daylight. Neither he nor Maya had seen any cars or trucks on the road. They assumed she was practicing her endurance running for the Sunrise Ceremony. They didn't become alarmed until a couple of hours after sunset.

"I'm glad you brought it up. I also need some information about the Sunrise Ceremony," said Zeb.

Just outside the sheriff's private enclosure, Helen's chair squeaked as she moved into position for an earful. Zeb rose from his chair, hitched his pants, walked around his desk and started to shut his office door. There was a time and place for Helen's eavesdropping. This wasn't one of them.

"Helen," he said, "this is going to take a while. Would you please hold all my calls?"

The sheriff turned the knob, closing the door soundlessly.

"About the Sunrise Ceremony, can you help me?"

"What do you want to know?" asked Song Bird.

"That's the problem. I don't exactly know what I want to know. I don't even know what I need to know. I was hoping you could help me with that."

"Let me put it this way then," said Song Bird. "What do you know about the Sunrise Ceremony?"

"That's just it, I don't know a thing about it," said Zeb. "You could say I'm steeped in ignorance."

"Why do you want to know about the Sunrise Ceremony? You're not planning on arresting anyone for performing the Sunrise Ceremony, are you?" asked Song Bird.

"No, why would I arrest someone for that?"

"Because it's against the law, that's why. Since the early part of this century, the US government has formally banned all Apache girls from performing the ceremony. Federal laws call the Sunrise Ceremony 'a spiritual act, ritualistic in nature and an act of defiance against a Christian nation'. Not to sound like some sort of a radical, but according to your lawmakers in Washington, partaking in such traditional observances, even after the American Indian Religious Freedom Act, is strongly discouraged."

"That sounds to me like a federal problem," said Zeb, "not a local one. I can assure you I have no intention of interfering with the private, religious ceremonies of the tribe. I think you know that."

It dawned on Zeb that the information he was asking for fell into the sacred and privileged category. He was banking on the long-standing trust between the two of them for Song Bird to be forthcoming.

"Long ago, the elders," began Song Bird, "in their wisdom to keep the Apache culture alive, took the ceremony underground. Because of the potential problem of being arrested for taking part in one of our sacred rites, the Sunrise Ceremony was performed in total secrecy for almost a hundred years. Today, some families are choosing to bring it back into the public eye, which I am uncertain is the right thing to do."

The sheriff was startled by the striking similarity between

Song Bird's story of religious persecution and the stories Zeb's grandparents and parents had told him about his Mormon ancestors.

"Why do you really want to know about the ceremony?" asked Song Bird.

"Let's just say I have a hunch that knowledge of the Sunrise Ceremony might help with your granddaughter's murder investigation," said Zeb.

"I'll help as much as I can, but there are many things about the ceremony I don't know," said Song Bird.

"As an Elder of the San Carlos and as its Medicine Man, I assumed you knew all the rituals."

"Some things are kept secret, even from me," said Song Bird.

"Can I ask why?"

"The Sunrise Ceremony is not my turf because it's a ceremony that the women of the tribe handle."

"Tell me what you can," said Zeb.

"Na'ii'ees," began Song Bird.

"What?" begged Zeb.

"Na'ii'ees, that's the Apache name for the Sunrise Ceremony. It's a unique and special ceremony. It is for girls only."

"Why girls only?"

Zeb's question brought softness to the tired, serious look on Song Bird's face.

"It's a ceremony only for girls because it celebrates the first flowing of their womanhood."

"Flowing of their womanhood?" asked Zeb.

"Menstruation."

Zeb's cheeks reddened with embarrassment.

"During the Na'ii'ees, mountain spirits, called g'ans by my people, appear. The g'ans inspire numerous sacred ceremonies, dances and songs. Their power helps us to perform ancient, traditional reenactments of the original ways with the proper virtue. One of the most important parts of the sacred rite is when the girls become imbued with the physical and spiritual power of White Painted Woman."

"Who is White Painted Woman?" asked the sheriff.

"White Painted Woman is like Eve in the Christian religion. She is the First Woman, the mother of the First People. We call her Esdzanadehe or Changing Woman. Her story is one of beauty and power. In modern times, educated people call the story an allegory. But all those who carry real Apache blood in their veins believe it as the literal truth. Our religion, like Christianity, also tells the story of the great flood. When the waters arose to cover the earth, the Changing Woman was the sole human survivor, having escaped the holocaust by stowing away inside an abalone shell."

"An abalone shell?" asked Zeb.

"Yes," said Song Bird. "Like the one found inside my granddaughter's chest."

Song Bird's forthrightness created a sense of heaviness in the room.

"If this is too difficult, we can talk later," said Zeb.

"No, it's okay. Let me continue. When the heavens ceased their downpour, she found herself among the highest mountaintops. There, as the water receded, she was impregnated by the sun and gave birth to a baby boy. This first son was called the Killer of Enemies. Soon after she was once again impregnated, this time by Rain. Her second child was called Son of Water."

"Whether the story is myth or truth, the first and second sons must be powerful representations to the Apache," mused Zeb.

"They are because they represent the safety of all the People. Both were born with a specific intent. Killer of Enemies and Son of Water, by the rite of their births, must kill the Owl Man Giant who has brought all this great terror. When they accomplish their mission, White Painted Woman, the Changing Woman, is waiting and expresses a cry of triumph and delight. This cry of victory is remembered through all time. During the Sunrise Ceremony, this joyous refrain will be echoed by the godmother."

"The godmother?"

"The godmother is the stand-in for the White Painted Woman. She is a mentor chosen by the family of the girl and will assist the soon-to-be woman in preparation for the Sunrise Ceremony as well as becoming her lifelong role model. The godmother is blessed and guided by spirits to establish a puberty rite for the girl. It is her responsibility to instruct the women of the tribe in the ritual and rites of womanhood."

"What happens to White Painted Woman?"

"You ask good questions, Zeb. Maybe one day we'll make you an honorary Apache...Apache woman, that is."

Surprised by Song Bird's ability to become lighthearted, Zeb managed an awkward grin.

"She becomes old, as we all do. However, when she gets old, she walks east toward the sun until she meets her younger self. When the old woman meets with the young woman, they merge, and White Painted Woman becomes young again. She lives from generation to generation with this rebirth," said Song Bird.

"Where does the young girl fit into this ceremony?"

"She learns about being a woman," said Song Bird. "Through ceremony and mentoring she gains a greater understanding of the physical manifestations of womanhood such as menstruation. But she also becomes aware of the physical endurance, inner strength and power of sexuality that lives inside women. Of course, all of this comes only after rigorous physical training for the ceremony which helps her endure the four long days and nights of almost continual running, dancing and praying."

"Running and dancing for four days?" asked Zeb. "I doubt I could have done that in my prime. Pardon me for saying so, but it seems almost brutal."

"To someone unaware of the power of Apache tradition, it might seem so. But you must stop and try to understand the symbolic and real power that comes with running in the four directions and becoming aware of the four stages of life. These girls are blessed to be able to pass through the sacred gate of womanhood and receive all the gifts and blessings associated with it. During the ceremony, prayers and heartfelt wishes for prosperity, wellbeing, fruitfulness, and a long and healthy life are bestowed upon them by the tribe. And ultimately, while becoming a woman is the purpose of the tradition, the re-enactment of the creation myth connects the girl to her spiritual heritage and allows her to find her core. We believe the girl-woman's true nature is found in this innermost of spirits. She finds her own spiritual power, sacredness and goodness. With this ancient knowledge that is new to her, she gains command over her weaknesses and especially the dark forces of her nature."

"What dark forces can possibly be in a young girl?" asked Zeb.

"The same dark forces that dwell in everyone. The ill omens of moral corruption," responded Song Bird. "Have you never wrestled with the force inside of you that commands your evil side?"

Zeb saw his reflected image in the wise man's eyes. Of course he had felt the power of evil rise inside of him. All men wrestle with the feeling in extreme circumstances. He thought of the time in Tucson when he nabbed a killer who had strangled his own mother. Zeb would have killed him if his partner hadn't stopped him.

"Do you believe the nature of evil is as omnipotent as the power of good?"

"Throughout all time, good and evil are also at continual odds," replied Song Bird.

Song Bird paused, bringing the hot coffee to his lips, allowing the pensive Zeb some time to mull over this new concept.

"Four days of rigorous physical activity, sexual maturation, prayers, rituals, the four directions," repeated Zeb. "It's all a strange, new way of thinking for me. But as foreign as it is, it somehow makes sense."

"Yes," said Song Bird.

"But the nature of evil being undeniably present in an innocent child? I'm not sure I buy that. Do you really think there are dark forces in every Apache girl?" asked Zeb.

"My people are one hundred percent certain dark forces reside in everyone. They are present from the time of birth. The Sunrise Ceremony helps the girl who is becoming a woman to rid herself of the evil side of her nature."

"Like baptism purifies the soul and removes the stain of original sin?" asked Zeb.

"Our cultures are less different than you might think."

The Medicine Man's words clarified the killer's motivation in the sheriff's mind. He was becoming certain he was dealing with the same person in the deaths of Amanda Song Bird and Angel Bright. Both victims were in the process of using traditional methods, one Mormon, one Apache, to symbolically purge evil from their souls. The killer's motivation was to see that transition halted.

"Song Bird, there's something you should know. I don't want our conversation going any further than it absolutely has to. You know how the rumor mill works. If what I'm about to tell you gets around, there's a damn good chance someone will take justice into their own hands. Innocent people could get hurt, maybe even killed. Worse yet, if the killer were to get wind of what we know, he might leave the area once and for all and never be found."

The old Medicine Man remained stoic and resolute as the sheriff told him that the killer of Angeline Bright had placed a Book of Mormon, inscribed with a message to Jake Dablo, in her chest where her heart had been.

"I'm convinced, and so is Jake, that the killer of Angel Bright and your granddaughter are one and the same person. I also believe the killer is insane."

"I can tell you that the superstitious sorts on the reservation would agree with you. They are blaming evil spirits and the Gods of the underworld."

The familiar cadence of his secretary's knuckles halted the conversation.

"Come in, Helen," said the sheriff.

"Sorry, Sheriff. I hate to interrupt, but there's a man on the phone who's insisting on talking to you."

"Who is it?" asked Sheriff Hanks.

Helen paused, glancing toward Song Bird whose back was turned to her. The implication was obvious. Could she speak freely in front of the Apache Medicine Man?

"Who is it?" reiterated the sheriff.

"A Mr. Benjamin Jensen. He's a private investigator from Phoenix. Something about a missing person."

"I'll take it," said the sheriff.

"Please keep me informed if you bring in any suspects. I would like to know," said Song Bird.

"I'll see that you're informed right away," said Zeb. "I don't think it will take long. I think I'm beginning to understand how this killer works and why he operates the way he does."

"Be careful," said Song Bird. "Often things are not as they seem to be."

Zeb pondered Song Bird's odd parting statement as the old man ambled out his office door.

The sheriff picked up the phone. "This is Sheriff Zeb Hanks."

"Thanks for taking my call, Sheriff Hanks," replied the detective.

"What can I help you with?"

"I'll be in Safford tomorrow. I was hoping you could make some time in your busy schedule for me."

Having worked with private investigators when he was a detective in Tucson had taught Zeb cooperating with them was often as much trouble as not. But this wasn't Tucson, and the politics in Safford weren't the same as those in the big city.

"What do you need to see me about?" asked the sheriff.

"A missing person," replied the detective.

"You think they might be found in Graham County."

"Possibly. You know of a place called Red's Roadhouse?"

"Yup."

"Good, that helps. Are you friendly with the powers that be out on the reservation? I mean, if they have a problem they can't solve on their own, do they ever come to you?" asked Jensen.

"Are you talking about something specifically?" asked the sheriff.

"I don't know for certain. It's just something that I dug up that looks a little funny to me. But I'd rather not talk about it on the phone."

"Be at my office at noon. I'll make some time for you then."

"I'll be there at twelve sharp tomorrow. We'll talk then. Goodbye."

Sheriff Hanks glanced at his slightly open office door and called out.

"Helen, do you have any idea what that detective wants?"

"Not really. He didn't say anything other than it was a missing person's case. He seemed like sort of a hush hush kind of guy to me."

"That's not what I mean, Helen. I mean have you heard about anything that might bring a private detective to town?"

Helen would have the low down on any mischief that might have passed him by.

"The murder of that child up on the reservation, I suppose. I assumed that the Song Bird clan had hired him."

"Song Bird would have told me if he were going to do that. Anything else out on the reservation that you've heard any gossip about?"

"No, not really. Not lately," replied Helen.

"How about a while ago? Did you hear something then?"

"A couple of things. There were some stories going around that the Catholic Church is buying up a bunch of Apache holy land on Mount Graham to put in a retreat for alcoholic priests."

"That one's not true. I checked it out myself."

"The only other thing is, well, I'm sure it's nothing. A couple of times a year, going back, oh I suppose fifteen or twenty years, some young person from the tribe who's moved off the reservation and up to Phoenix or over to Tucson is found dead. An old Apache woman named Mrs. Trudy Feathers, she's in my sewing circle, was talking about it."

"That happens all the time. Young Indians move to the big city and get involved with the wrong sort of people and end up dead. Drugs and violence are a lot more common up there than down here."

"She knows that too. And she didn't find it at all odd that young people got killed in the big city, what with all the violence and everything that goes on. It's just that for about five or six years no one was killed. Then, suddenly, it started up again a couple of years ago. And just like in the past, it always happens in June and December, late in the month."

"Does Mrs. Feathers have any theories on why it happens this way?"

"She says all she knows is that it's the work of the devil. I agree with her one hundred percent."

"How about Red's Roadhouse? He was asking about that, too. Have you heard anything recently about that place?"

"That den of iniquity, just about anything could happen in such an apocalyptic place. I wouldn't be surprised should Satan himself show up there one day."

Helen's adamant manner brought a smile to Zeb's face. He glanced at the stack of paperwork on his desk and felt the pangs of an instant headache creeping up the back of his neck. It was too early for lunch, and he had skipped breakfast. He diagnosed the discomfort as a hunger pain.

"I'm going over to the Town Talk for a late breakfast. You can reach me there if you need me."

"All right, Sheriff. Bring me one of Doreen's special blueberry muffins, would you?" asked Helen.

"Of course. I wouldn't want to deny you and your sweet tooth," said Zeb with a wink.

"Couldn't be you're headed in that direction to pick up a little sugar yourself, could it, Sheriff?" asked Helen.

Zeb paused. He was either wearing his heart on his sleeve or rumors were already spreading about him and Doreen. No matter, keeping a secret from Helen was not part of the equation.

"One blueberry muffin comin' up," he said, heading out the door.

14

At the cafe, the proprietor greeted the sheriff with her usual sass.

"I wasn't expectin' the likes of a handsome feller like yerself 'til at least lunch time, Sheriff. What's the matter, you miss lil' ol' Doe already?"

Of course he did, but he had no idea how to express it. He had quietly had his eye on her for most of five years and many times considered moving forward with the courting process. But like any man inexperienced and unlearned in the ways of women, he waited for her to make the first move.

"I miss you a little bit every day," he mumbled under his breath.

The sheriff could scarcely believe his ears upon hearing his own utterance. Those simple and true words, *miss you every day*, were said with real meaning, just the way a man should talk to a woman like Doreen. Such tender, straightforward words from the mouth of Zeb Hanks set the usually brassy Doreen spinning for a loop.

"You all right, hon'? You runnin' a fever? Maybe you was tick bit?"

Doreen placed her wrist against the sheriff's forehead and then tested against her own.

"You sure don't feel like your engine's about to boil over."

Zeb, already discombobulated by his hunger headache, was more than a little flustered. At a loss for words, he fiddled nervously with the spoon in front of him. Doreen smiled and poured some sugar in his coffee, brushing her hand against his in the process.

"Must be hunger workin' in at ya, then? What can I get for you, big man? The usual?" asked Doreen.

"Yah, well, why don't you cook me up a couple of eggs, poached medium, with white toast and a big side of western style potatoes?"

"Did I hear you say western spuds?" asked a wide-eyed Doreen. "Puttin' a little spice in your life, huh big fella?"

"Giving it some serious consideration," replied Zeb.

"Careful where you're drawin' a bead, big shooter. You ain't got no idea what sorta trouble you're aimin' your six-shooter at."

The swelling in his heart rose faster than the flame rising under the fry pan that was cooking up one Western Special.

Doreen brought him the food, refilled his coffee cup and took a seat next to him. Gently massaging his neck, she offered him comfort.

"It's about that murder out on the San Carlos, ain't it? The murder of that poor little girl?" asked Doreen. "That's drivin' ya' loco, ain't it?"

The coffee and neck rub erased what was left of his headache, and the food quelled his nausea.

"It's a real bad deal, you know," said Zeb. "That's not the kind of thing that should ever happen anywhere, much less right here in the heart of Graham County."

Doreen felt the broad shoulder muscles of the big man beginning to loosen.

"You got any suspects?" she asked.

"Not yet, but we're working on it."

Doreen whispered secretively, even though the few people in the Town Talk were seated nowhere near them.

"Is the scuttlebutt I been hearin' on the grapevine true?"

"I suppose that depends on what you've been hearing," said Zeb.

"Don't tell me the latest gossip hasn't fallen on your ears, Zeb Hanks. I mean, the whole town's a yakkin' over it."

"Talking about what?"

"Folks are sayin' it was them space aliens that cut that poor little girl all to pieces. There's talk they opened her up and did experiments on her. Just like you read about in them magazines they sell over at Links Grocery. I don't rightly believe everything I read in them rags, but you never know. And there have been all those UFO sightings down by Lordsburg."

"People have a tendency to let their imaginations run freely, Doreen."

"Sure they do. Who's sayin' they don't?"

"Not me," replied Zeb. "All I'm saying is that when one person says something and two other people hear it and they tell two people...well, pretty soon the whole town is taking gossip for the truth."

"I suppose it gets around like that. But how do you explain away all them cattle mutilations that have been goin' on down New Mexico way?" asked Doreen.

"Rustlers," replied Zeb.

"Zeb Hanks, you expect one person in a hundred to believe a rustler's gonna risk his neck just to cut out the internal organs of some dumb ol' cow? The fool that's dumb enough to do that sort of thing and leave all the good meat behind wouldn't be no kind of rustler I ever heard of. What do you take me for anyway? Do I look like I was born yesterday?"

"I never implied that, Doreen. But you do have to be careful about believing those sorts of rumors. Like I said, that's how stories get started."

"Rumors, schmoozers. What I do know is what people are talkin' about and how people think."

"And how's that?"

"If aliens are cuttin' up cattle for experiments and just takin' certain parts out of 'em, why not do the same to people? Tell me that ain't logical!"

"It ain't...isn't," said Zeb. "Mostly because all those rumors about cattle organs missing are just that—rumors."

"Just cause it's a rumor don't mean it ain't true," said Doreen.

"Speaking of rumors, any hot ones making the rounds about the reservation?"

"There's a lot of talk that there's people out there who know exactly what happened to that poor lil' child. But they're keepin' mum. You know, Indian secrecy and all that."

"Not too many folks can keep that big of a secret, Doe. At least not for long."

"Up there they do. Those reservation folks, they tend to keep the bad things that happen on their own turf to themselves. And there are some real crazy Apaches out there. Everyone knows that."

"There's real crazy people everywhere," said Zeb, "both White and Indian alike."

"I got nothing against them Apaches. Personally, I'm hopin' it's an outsider that done such a horrible thing. So, if you ain't got no suspects, what exactly are you doin' to keep our fair city safe?"

"It's my job to find out who the killer is and arrest him. That's exactly what I'm working on. After that, it's the job of the court system to see that justice is done. I'm sure it all will happen in due time," said Zeb.

"The sooner the better, I'd say! We sure don't want no killer walkin' around free."

"I couldn't agree with you more, Doe."

Doreen reached over and kneaded the sheriff's muscles vigorously. After a few moments, she squared the shoulders of his uniform and cleared away his plate.

"That headache of yours a little better, sugar dumplin'?" she asked.

"It's nothing but a distant memory, Doe. I think the aliens took it away on their spaceship."

"Oh hush your mouth," said Doreen.

Smacking him gently on the back of the head, she got up and sashayed around the corner of the lunch counter. The swaying of her hips in her spotless, white uniform caught Zeb's eye, making him tingle in all the right places.

"How do you do it, Doreen?"

Doreen swept her hair away from her face with a flick of the wrist, exposing a smile that could light the way out of any man's darkness.

"Whatever are you talkin' about, Sheriff?"

"How do you stay so perfect?"

"That's awful nice of you to say, Zeb, but I'm darn near the farthest thing from perfection, 'cept to a man with stars in his eyes."

Amidst a palpable silence, Doreen pulled the clips from her up do, allowing it to fall over her shoulders. Leaning forward across the counter, she whispered to Zeb.

"However, Mr. Zeb Hanks, you can just keep on believin' whatever your lil' heart desires."

Letting her eyelid close in a sultry wink, Doreen swung around and pranced her way through the swinging kitchen doors. Zeb was transfixed on her every titillating motion. He perked his ears as he listened to Doreen croon softly. He couldn't quite place the tune, but the rhythm told him it was definitely a love song.

Zeb grabbed a couple of muffins and left a large tip. As he turned to tip his hat to the radiantly beaming Doreen, the buoyancy in his step induced by the sparkle in her expression caused him to slam a shoulder into the door frame. Zeb casually brushed aside the pain and embarrassment. He headed for the office where he dropped off Helen's treats before driving up to Antelope Flats to have another look at the scene of the crime.

15

The trip north on Highway 70 to the death scene went by quickly. Sheriff Hanks barely noticed the scenery as he mulled over his new information and knowledge.

Song Bird's and Jake's granddaughters both being in preparation for a religious rite stuck in Zeb's craw. The abalone shell in Amanda's chest and the Book of Mormon placed in Angel's made it clear the killer had at least a working knowledge of Mormon and Native religions. But that could be a ruse intended to misguide him. What seemed more likely to Zeb was a tie to the mothers, Jenny and Maya. They had been best friends who hung out with some very dangerous characters. Maybe they had crossed the same person who had exacted revenge against their daughters. Although the sheriff's office routinely received reports of UFO sightings, Doreen's silly gossip about the alien abductions was right out of the rag magazines. Toss in a little of Mrs. Trudy Feathers' theory about the timing of dead young Apaches off the reservation and a detective coming to town about some mysterious missing person, and you could find yourself embroiled in a fine fettle.

At the scene of the murder, Zeb found things exactly as he

had left them. The site felt incredibly lonely and remote. Sitting at the center of the five candles, he took off his hat and carefully placed it on the ground behind him. Eyelids closed, the sheriff shut out the visual world. A gentle breeze rushed across his neck, cooling it, relaxing him. Lying on his back, he stared into the blue sky focusing on the passing clouds. Zeb closed his eyes and drifted off into a deep sleep. An hour later he was awakened by the grinding engine of an approaching truck. As he got up, Tommy Horse Legs stepped out of an Apache police truck.

"I saw dust trails when you drove up here a while back," said Horse Legs.

Zeb looked at his watch. He hadn't realized how much time had passed.

"When you didn't make the trip down the hill, I decided I'd better come up and have a look. Everything all right?"

"Just having another look around."

Zeb replaced his hat on his head. Horse Legs stood in awkward silence until the tribal officer made a stab at small talk.

"You're the first person to come by this way since you were here last time. It's been kind of lonely out here. Gives a man plenty of time to think."

"Officer Horse Legs?"

"Yes, sir."

"Can I be direct with you?"

"Yes, sir."

"Do you think an Apache or a White killed Song Bird's granddaughter?"

"A White killed her. I can tell you that in no uncertain terms."

"How can you be so positive?"

"All the signs point to it."

"Signs?"

"Her hands, Sheriff. They were sort of stuffed inside her

body when we found her. I know for certain an Apache would never do something like that."

"How do you know that?"

"No Apache would ever touch a dead body. It stands to reason that whoever stuck her hands inside the wounds could only have done it after she was dead. And no Apache would stick their hands inside a living body to begin with. You ever see an Apache surgeon? There aren't any."

"How about a renegade? What about someone who had moved off the reservation and wasn't living the Apache way?"

"Well, maybe that could happen, but I doubt it."

"But the possibility exists."

"There was a second thing that makes me certain a White did it. It was the way they tried to sew the hands into her chest cavity. I saw it close up. That wasn't Apache stitching. It was nothing but big broad loops. Apache stitches are small and fine. I wouldn't waste any more of your time looking on the Rez. The killer isn't one of us."

Sheriff Hanks thanked the tribal deputy. He returned to Safford thinking about what Horse Legs had said. The pile of paperwork on his desk seemed to have grown in his absence. Hunched over his undersized desk, Sheriff Hanks didn't look up again until the grandfather clock in the front office chimed a dozen times. The final hours before midnight had slipped past in what seemed like a few short minutes. Fatigued, Zeb rubbed the tips of his fingers roughly against his temples, hoping to stimulate his tired brain. Flecks of dry skin fell from his scalp, filtering through the air, landing on the scattered pages of what was now called the Antelope Flats murder file.

By Sheriff Hanks' order, the murder case of Amanda Song Bird was officially the Antelope Flats murder case, in deference to the respect the Native culture gave to their dead. Song Bird had taught him long ago that it was customary practice among the Apache to avoid speaking the name of the dead. Uttering the name of the recently deceased, it was believed, impeded their passage into the spirit world. The same divination held true for touching their personal belongings. Horse Legs had made it very clear, since laying a hand upon the corpse was virtually unheard of, a genuine Apache would never place an object inside a dead person. He cursed himself for not having put it together from the start. The killer was not an Apache and, for sure, Song Bird suspected the same, yet he said nothing.

Zeb was puzzled why Song Bird would tell him about the Sunrise Ceremony, which constituted a leap of faith, one that hurdled the chasm that separated the old ways from the new, yet failed to point out something as obvious as what Horse Legs had mentioned. In addition, by allowing the autopsy of his granddaughter, Song Bird was defying traditional mores, leaving him wide open for potentially serious repercussions from fellow tribal members. The implications were enormous. It was clear the highly respected Medicine Man was using a different standard when it came to his own family.

Sheriff Hanks intertwined his fingers behind his head and leaned back in his chair. As the second hand ticked away the minutes on the old clock, he thought of how people referred to the death of Angeline Bright. Rarely did anyone refer to her directly. Instead people merely mentioned "October eighteenth" or "the murder of Sheriff Dablo's granddaughter." The failure to mention her name was a cultural similarity he had overlooked. Now, the same thing was happening all over again. The death of Amanda Song Bird was referred to as "that poor little Apache girl who was killed up at Antelope Flats." The sheriff looked down at her printed name and respectfully avoided saying it aloud. But what he couldn't do was avoid the echo in his head of *Amanda Song Bird...Amanda Song Bird...Amanda Song Bird.* The more he tried to stop it, the louder the mantra repeated itself. Through blurry eyes, he read the autopsy report one more time.

The coldly scientific description of the incision into the child's flesh and excision of her heart in Dr. Virant's report triggered a fire bolt of electricity rippling up his spine. In his hands was the final chapter of a human life that had ended in torture and violence. Yet the doctor's report was void of emotion. He felt his face turn red as he seethed in anger. For the sake of Song Bird and Maya there needed to be resolution. The only just ending to the story would be the death penalty for the killer. But that wouldn't happen. No jury in Arizona would pass that kind of a penalty on a person who committed an act this insane.

Zeb's body tingled as though his head had been injected with Novocain. His office suddenly seemed inordinately quiet as a deep shiver fought its way through the numbness. When Amanda Song Bird's name became synchronous with the beating of his heart, Sheriff Hanks was overwhelmed. He realized this murder case now carried its own, distinct rhythm and it was pulsating inside him.

He organized his notes, touching each page, waiting in vain for an answer to jump off the paper at him. He needed a breakthrough, someone willing to step forward, an event to happen that would propel him nearer the killer. A single chime on the clock reminded him that another hour had passed. He rubbed his eyes and placed the newly ordered file in the top drawer of his desk. Taking a deep breath, he realized that he was standing at the precipice of allowing this murder to become personal. He pushed himself away from his desk, donned his hat and walked outside into the cool night air.

Standing on the front steps of the office, he gazed at the crescent moon. The twinkling stars served as a background to its radiance. As the moonbeams struck Zeb's face and calmed him, he recalled a lesson Jake had learned from his grandfather and graciously passed on. The story contained a bit of wisdom from an older generation of cowboys who seemed able to toss out such tidbits with each spit of their chewing tobacco.

Jake's grandfather had taught Jake that moonlight has the power to make men forget, if only for a fleeting moment, the seriousness of living a day-to-day existence. When you stare at the moon, if you listen closely enough, you can hear the sweet music moonbeams carry through the atmosphere. How many old lonesome cowboys, Zeb wondered, had the moon helped release their worldly woes?

Squinting at the stars, Zeb imagined a formation that appeared as a noose hanging from a tree. His tired mind saw it slowly slipping around the neck of the killer. "Quick justice at the end of rope," Jake used to say, "it's not perfect justice, but it has its place."

Amanda Song Bird...Amanda Song Bird. In the soft, pale aura of the moonlight, her name repeated itself like a cool breeze on a chilly desert night. A beautiful young girl viciously murdered on the cusp of traditional womanhood. Why? The death of any child, even a natural one, made no sense. The murder of an innocent young person leapt across the border of sanity. Zeb knew he had to think like the killer, get inside his head. Yet, how could he when there was no way to even justify the existence of such hideous thoughts?

If Song Bird or Maya made a vicious enemy along the way, that person may now be exacting his pound of flesh in the most revengeful manner. Maybe Horse Legs had it backwards. Maybe only an Apache could do such a thing, thereby creating the perfect alibi.

Zeb felt hot, as though the moonbeams were heating him with the power of mid-afternoon sunshine. He erased the cool beads of midnight sweat from his forehead with a heavy hand. In the distance, near the graveyard at the edge of town, he listened to the cry of a stray coyote. Zeb shuddered with the thought that no matter the race of the killer, Apache or White, he was dealing with a rabid, lone wolf. And right at this moment the lunatic was moving freely about his county. If Zeb didn't find him soon, God only knew what the consequences might be and who would be next.

October eighteenth, the date was everywhere. He saw it on the office calendar, in Helen's handwriting underlined three times and on the autopsy reports of Amanda Song Bird and Angeline Bright. He saw it in the stars. Why October eighteenth? Why had the killer chosen that date? His eyes once again shifted toward the heavens. This time the stars were a painting he had seen in art class in high school. He searched his memory for the name and laughed aloud at its obviousness as it came back to him. *Starry, Starry Night.* Vincent Van Gogh was the artist. A dreamy skyscape painted by an artist who lopped off his own ear in a fit of madness.

"A mad man," Zeb said aloud. "How do you find a madman? Where does a madman hide?" He inhaled deeply through his nostrils and exhaled slowly through his mouth. Sheriff Hanks knew that finding such a person demanded that he think like a madman. His head began to throb.

Zeb blinked a few times, stretched his neck and gazed across the desert toward the horizon. A shooting star arced into oblivion as a single truck passed, heading south through town. It was then he noticed that the streets of Safford were unnaturally quiet. The city, like the surrounding desert, should have been coming to life by this time of night. The lawman had been trained to observe activity. Inactivity allowed him no action steps and nothing to evaluate. Something was wrong, out of synch. For a moment, he was uncertain if it was the world or just himself.

Taking a spin around town, he sought out the turf of low

lifers, driving by their homes and hangouts. But tonight, the bad parts of town were as quiet as the inside of a Monday night church. Not even the Lopez gang or the Garcia brothers were out and about. The peacefulness grated his mind, making him uncomfortably suspicious.

Sheriff Hanks drove home in a restless, angry mood. He lay down on the sofa and switched on the television, keeping the volume one notch lower than normal. His house, extraordinarily quiet like the rest of Safford, held no solace.

The slumber that sneaked over him carried him fitfully to the three o'clock hour when the low, static hum of white noise from an off-the-air television station startled him into a slow wake. Stiff in the lower back from sleeping on the worn sofa cushions, he stood and stretched his arms overhead, brushing a hand against the slowly rotating ceiling fan. The dull blade scuffed his knuckle, opening a small laceration. Instinctively, he licked the wound. The metallic tang of blood wakened him fully.

Alert, he pulled back the shade and peered out the window. An old car with one tail light missing moved slowly up the street. When it parked, he shut the curtain. Out of habit, he listened for a door slam. When none came, he figured it was a polite night shift worker, not wanting to wake his family, quietly shutting the car door as he arrived home at the very late hour. Still dressed in his work clothes, Zeb walked to his bed and lay down on top of the crumpled covers. Moments later he fell asleep and drifted off to a land fertile with dreams.

In his dream, he saw Doreen Nightingale straddling her blue Electra Glide Harley Davidson. As she sped through the open desert at full throttle, he felt the power of his own Harley between his legs humming against the pavement. Glancing in her direction, Doreen responded with a serene smile. Even in the dream state he felt her gaze push him deeper into a cloud of tranquil clarity. Mesmerized, his eyes caught the trail of an eagle flying behind her in the low desert. Doreen's long hair, flying straight back in the warm wind, seemed to swallow the large bird.

"Doreen," he mouthed. "Your hair is magical."

As he spoke, a face, half-hidden in Doreen's hair, flowed mysteriously into the body of a passenger who was clinging to the driver. The gentle whipping movement of her tresses prevented him from getting a clear view of the rider until the wind finally brushed her locks aside. The sheriff was stunned when he saw that the co-rider was a young Indian girl. Smiling and laughing as she rode through the desert carefree and euphoric, she somehow passed on harmonious vibrations to Zeb. He was taken aback with the realization of who the passenger was. The beautiful young passenger was Amanda Song Bird.

The graceful child smiled innocently. She seemed to be waiting for him to catch her eye. When he did, Amanda slowly raised her arm and directed his line of sight to the soaring eagle. As it swooped low, fanning its magnificent wings to slow its airspeed and land, the eagle clasped its sharp, golden talons atop a monument in a graveyard. Zeb watched in awe as it took off as quickly as it landed. In its place, standing in front of the monument, was an apparition robed like the grim reaper. He watched, spellbound, as Doreen's motorcycle entered the cemetery and roared up to the pallid figure. In a moment of lucid dreaming, Zeb shouted to Doreen to run the apparition over, to kill it. Instead, Doreen parked the Harley only feet away from the evil being. Her passenger, Amanda Song Bird, got off the motorcycle and joined the harbinger of death who suddenly had taken the human personification of Angel Bright. Within the dream his eyesight focused on the girls' faces. A lapis and gold necklace around Amanda's neck shimmered in the sun. A beautiful onyx cameo graced Angel's neck. Zeb shot up in his bed, drenched with sweat and gasping for air.

He told himself he wasn't superstitious and that he didn't believe in dreams as omens. His head was flooded with a thousand thoughts that contradicted his long-held convictions.

16

Tired from lack of sleep, strange dreams and a belief system that seemed fractured and riddled with inconsistencies, the sheriff arrived at his office. Eskadi Black Robes was seated by Helen's desk waiting for him.

With a minimal movement of his head, Zeb directed his guest to the chair in front of his desk.

"What I've got is exactly nothing. In fact, things are so quiet on the reservation, it's almost eerie."

"It was a long shot, but I was hoping you'd find something that would help me."

"No such luck, but I did talk with Song Bird last night," said Eskadi. "He said he would talk with you if you had any more questions. It's okay if we stop by this morning."

"Good. We should."

Zeb looked up at the big circular clock hanging on the wall. It chimed half past the hour. The timing couldn't be better. He would make a quick run up to Wildhorse Canyon. He could talk with Song Bird more about the case and, while it was still fresh in his mind, ask him about his dream. He would still have no trouble being back for his noon meeting with the detective.

"Let's get cracking," said Zeb, picking up his car keys. "I'll follow you up there."

The small caravan of two official vehicles, one a BIA truck and the other a Graham County Dodge Dakota pickup, met little traffic on the highway and none on the dirt road leading to Wildhorse Canyon. The serene beauty of the vast emptiness helped Zeb calm the overhanging angst associated with his haunting dream.

As the men pulled into the driveway, Zeb noticed Song Bird sitting beneath an ancient, gnarly mesquite. The tree's shadows, interwoven with patches of sunlight, made the tribal elder appear almost as one with his natural surroundings. A brightly colored mourning feather, held loosely in his hand, seemed to float on the air. A gust of wind roiled up a little dust, further obscuring the old Indian's presence.

Song Bird faced in the direction of the rising sun, motionless. He took no notice of his visitors as they got out of the car. His head, tipped slightly toward the earth, appeared to be bowed in prayer. A pair of red-beaked, broad-billed hummingbirds flitted inches above his head, taking off and landing in the branches of an overgrown bird of paradise bush.

Eskadi positioned himself on the bumper of his truck. With a silent hand signal, he beckoned the sheriff to join him. Zeb sat down next to him, turning up the collar of his light jacket as protection against the cool morning breeze. Eskadi, in his short-sleeved shirt, seemed unaffected by the temperature as he stared off to the east. Leaning against the warmed grill of the truck, the men remained still and quiet so as not to disturb the holy man. A quarter of an hour passed before Song Bird nimbly arose from the ground and came over to greet the men.

"Hon Dah," said Song Bird.

Eskadi returned the traditional greeting.

"Good morning, Zeb," said Song Bird.

"Good morning, Song Bird."

"Come inside," said Song Bird.

The two men followed the old man through a low door on the southern side of the house. He motioned them to have a seat around the hand-hewn kitchen table. With its four slatted chairs, it took up the front half of the house. On the table a variety of dried herbs and roots garnished a well-traveled mortar and pestle set. Behind the kitchen was a homey looking living room with a bed in the far corner. Next to a well-used fireplace was a ragged overstuffed chair that carried a perfect indentation of the Medicine Man's buttocks. A homemade shelf above the chair held a display of photographs. Overhead, a single dusty light bulb was the only source of artificial light. An aromatic blend of sage and pine wafting throughout the house gently stung Zeb's eyes.

Song Bird grabbed the pot of freshly brewed coffee from the stove and offered some to his guests. Eskadi politely declined, but Zeb gladly accepted.

"Most people shy away from my coffee," said Song Bird.

The sheriff watched as the old man poured what looked like black mud with interspersed flecks of green leaves into his cup. The dense, oily aroma of the coffee oddly complemented the lighter wafts of pine and sage.

"Most people don't care for real Apache coffee. Even some of our tribal leaders won't drink it," he said with a slight nod in Eskadi's direction. "I say it's only the spoiled, big city Apaches who prefer the white man's skinny water. They have forgotten how to drink the real thing."

The twinkle in Song Bird's eye and his good humor were encouraging signs. Perhaps the Medicine Man's heart really was beginning to mend. If so, he would be imminently approachable this morning.

Song Bird's response to the hurt and sorrow of his granddaughter's death was the antithesis of what Jake's had been. While Jake hid from the world and drowned his sorrows in hard liquor, Song Bird was working hard to restore a bit of normalcy to his life.

Zeb, Eskadi and Song Bird chatted about the oncoming winter and the increased activity of the animals as they prepared for the cold season. Zeb waited a respectful amount of time before bringing up the real reasons for his visit. He knew his timing fooled no one.

"Song Bird..."

The sheriff looked up to see the Medicine Man already peering deeply into his eyes. The deep crevices in the old Apache's face and the worldliness in his dark pupils revealed the life of a man who had survived dozens of battles and seen hundreds of changes of season.

"I know this isn't the best of times for you to answer some questions, but there are some things I need to know. I know it will be hard..."

Song Bird stopped the sheriff in mid-sentence by merely raising an eyebrow.

"Go ahead, Zeb. I want to help, and I am ready to speak. My pain is large, but the circle of life must continue. My prayers are for a new life to replace the one that has been lost. Ask me anything you want."

Zeb took a slug of Song Bird's so-called Apache coffee and nearly retched.

"You don't like my special blend?"

"It takes some getting used to."

"Like many things we face in this life," said Song Bird.

Realizing that, even in the midst of tragedy, humor and dignity were not lost on the old man made Zeb comfortable as he began his questioning.

"Every man has enemies..." began Zeb.

"Even the Gods have those who would fight against them," added Song Bird.

"But Eskadi tells me you believe that you have none. How can that be?"

"I think I may have outlived them all," said Song Bird. "After all, I am a very old man. Ancient in the eyes of young people. One young boy, when he heard I was a man of religion, asked me if I had met God and what he was like."

The wry smile on the old Indian's face hinted at a double meaning that was lost on the sheriff.

"After we talked yesterday I got to thinking that a man who has lived as long as I have may have picked up an enemy or two along the way without being aware of who they are. I have seen many men turn away from their fellow men and become evil. I have seen good men do bad things for no apparent reason. I can personally vouch that no man leads a perfect life."

As Song Bird's voice trailed off, Zeb was certain he observed a curious look in the eye of the Medicine Man. He couldn't quite place the look as one he had ever seen in Song Bird's eye. It struck him as uniquely odd in relation to the Medicine Man. It was the light, hazy glaze he had witnessed a thousand times in the eyes of men who were skirting the edge of the truth. Zeb listened intently, his suspicions roused that Song Bird might be hiding some small fact. He just couldn't be sure what he was hiding or why. Certainly a man like Song Bird could make enemies and never know it. A sly and cunning adversary would be wise to lay in wait for a long time, maybe even years, to seek revenge on such a powerful man as Song Bird. Zeb suspected the Medicine Man knew he had enemies and who they were. For some reason he wasn't speaking their names.

"Is it possible you have angered someone by your work as a Medicine Man?"

"Apaches honor Medicine Men."

As Song Bird spoke, the half-truth hidden in his eyes faded quickly.

"Besides, if I did a bad healing, the family would come and tell me so they could get their money back. Apaches are hard business people. They always want to get what they pay for. Let me tell you a story. One time Beualah Trees came to me when the ghost of a White man was bothering her by hanging around her house. For an Indian to be frightened by a White man's spirit is even worse than being scared by an Indian spirit. Worst of all, the ghost was that of the man who killed the man she was going to marry. It was a big predicament for everyone. It took me a long time. When I chased the ghost away, Beualah gave me enough canned goods to last a whole winter. But when the ghost decided to come back, she not only came and took the canned goods back, she also took my transistor radio and all my new candles. She said the music on the radio and the light from the candles were the only things that could protect her from the White man's ghost when it got dark outside. What could I do? I gave them to her willingly. But I can tell you this. If my medicine doesn't work, no one would want a life in return. They would want something material. They wouldn't want to create a ghost spirit that might come back to visit them."

"How about your daughter? Is there anyone you can think of who would wish her ill? Anyone who would harm her by hurting her daughter?"

"No one that I know of."

"Have you asked her?"

"She is in mourning. I won't disturb her until she has cleansed herself of the anger and confusion that comes with the loss of a child this way."

"How about your granddaughter's father?"

"He'd dead and gone. He never existed."

Song Bird's curt tone demanded Zeb quit probing in that

direction. The sheriff had heard on the Town Talk grapevine that, for some unknown reason, it was a very sore subject with Song Bird. The rumors as to why were many. None of them made sense to Zeb. But he added the dead girl's father to his short list of suspects.

Each question Zeb asked produced yet another dead end. His eyes scanned the inside of Song Bird's house, hoping to spot something that would trigger a greater understanding of the Apache way of thinking and a path behind the veil of Apache secrecy. On a shelf next to a picture of his daughter and granddaughter was a lapis and gold necklace. He reached for it when he felt Song Bird's hand on his shoulder.

"Do not touch it," he commanded.

Zeb drew back. Song Bird's eyes looked serious and pained.

"It is one of a set that was to be given by Maya to her daughter. She gave her the first one the day she disappeared. This is the second one, a gift that can never be given."

"I've seen the design somewhere before," said the sheriff.

Song Bird responded with a contemplative gaze that brought a silence to the small house. The quiet was interrupted by the sound of a dull thud against the glass. Eskadi, sitting near the window, peered out to see what had made the noise.

"Song Bird," said Eskadi. "Your window just killed a black and white striped woodpecker."

"It was no accident," said Song Bird. "The death of a ladder-backed woodpecker is a specific omen."

The Medicine Man reached over and lightly placed the palm of his hand on the sheriff's forehead. The action caused a strange sensation to permeate Zeb's body. He felt light, adrift, like he was floating in a pool of water.

"Tell me about your dream," said Song Bird.

Zeb was stunned by the mystical nature of the event. He rose from the chair, perplexed and feeling fiery hot where Song Bird had touched him. He raised his own hand to the spot but was stopped short by the Medicine Man's hand. Fear rushed through his body, but the calm look in the Medicine Man's eyes reassured him. He sat back down in the chair and slowly began to unfold the details of his dream.

"I saw your granddaughter riding on the back of Doreen Nightingale's motorcycle. Doreen is the woman who runs the café in town. I don't think she knew your granddaughter or your granddaughter knew her. They were flying down the highway, somewhere out in the desert, up near Morenci. Both of them were laughing and smiling. I remember clearly how Doreen's hair flying in the breeze hid your granddaughter's face. In my dream, I kept looking at her, curious as to who she was. Then, just before her face was made clear, an eagle swooped down and flew beside them, like he was playing with them or coming to greet them, maybe even guiding them. The dream made me feel very happy and peaceful until I woke up. Then I was afraid."

Additional segments of the dream came flooding back to him in intricate detail as he continued to recount it to Song Bird.

"The glint of the sun passing through the motorcycle's windshield caused Doreen and your granddaughter to squint, making their eyes tiny. Overhead, I could see pure white clouds moving in formation. As they moved from east to west, they became dark and ominous until lightening began shooting out from them. In the middle of the storm, I saw four men on horses pulling a chariot, like in an old biblical movie. Just below the clouds, the mountain peaks looked freshly painted in purple and bluish-pink. Below the peaks, the forest was dark green and heavily wooded with fir trees. Layers of scrub brush and saguaro cactus stirred slightly in the breeze. The landscape seemed to go on forever. Everything was so vivid. I remember seeing red lizards and rattlesnakes crawling in the sunlight along the rocks and sand. It was as if I'd never seen how much life there is in the desert before."

The rising sense of exhilaration that accompanied the sheriff's explanation was quickly replaced by an overwhelming sense of fatigue as he finished his story. Blinking several times, he felt that if he shut his eyes, he would instantly fall asleep.

"And the necklace," asked Song Bird, "was it in your dream, too?"

"Yes, I don't know why I forgot to mention it. Your granddaughter's necklace was hanging around her neck. When she was greeted by Jake's granddaughter, Angel was wearing a cameo necklace. They were hanging down across the girls' chests, directly over their..."

Zeb paused. His throat constricted as he spoke one final word.

"...hearts."

Song Bird arose from his place in the big chair and offered it to Zeb. Walking outside, Song Bird knelt near the fallen woodpecker. He carefully placed the small bird in the palm of his hand. Stroking its soft underbelly as he held it near his mouth, the Medicine Man whispered an incantation. Song Bird then carried it near the base of the ancient mesquite tree where he set it on the ground, covering it with leaves and grass.

Through the window, Eskadi and Zeb watched as Song Bird bowed to each of the four directions in prayer. At the end of the invocation, he reached into a small pouch and removed an offering of tobacco. An air of lightness surrounded him as he returned to his house and took a seat at the kitchen table.

"Your dream tells me my granddaughter is free. With the help of the Great Spirit and his watchers, she has quickly and joyously found her way to the spirit world. Your dream is powerful. It removes the sadness from my heart. I know, too, my daughter will be of better spirit when she hears of this."

Zeb was at a loss to understand how Song Bird had seen so clearly into his dream's meaning, yet happy to have played the part of an unwitting go-between. His body began to tingle. Brushing against the insight of the Medicine Man, he felt an indefinable, subtle shift in his perception. It was like he was witnessing the world through someone else's eyes.

"On the way to the spirit world, my granddaughter encountered the woman on the motorcycle, Doreen Nightingale. Do you know her well?"

"Yes, I know her," said Zeb.

"I would like very much to meet this woman. Would she come and talk to me, here?"

"I'll see," replied Zeb. "I think she will. I'll ask her."

"Tell her I would like her to come and see me. I want to thank her for what she has done," said Song Bird.

Looking revitalized and youthful, Song Bird walked to the corner of the living area and sat on the edge of the bed. He motioned Zeb to his side.

"The world has changed for you," he said. "This new knowledge you have gained will help you to serve others. It is difficult to open the eyes of an adult man, but I believe yours have been opened."

Zeb placed his hand into the Medicine Man's upturned palms and said goodbye.

Lying down, the old man closed his eyes and drifted instantly into what appeared to be a deep, peaceful sleep.

"He trusts you," said Eskadi. "You should believe in him and trust what he knows. His interpretation of your dream may help you solve the murders."

Zeb studied Eskadi's face and saw, for the first time, into his heart. He witnessed goodness and peace. He shook his head. Seeing Eskadi in this new light was going to take some getting used to.

Heading south on the highway toward Safford, Zeb replayed Eskadi's parting remarks in his head. His final comment, "your dream may help you solve the murders," kept echoing around his brain. Not *the murder* but, rather, *the murders*. Eskadi was also linking the murders of Amanda Song Bird and Angel Bright to the same person. But how could Eskadi be certain Song Bird's interpretation of Zeb's dream would have an impact on the case? How that would manifest itself was a mystery beyond his comprehension.

Cruising down the highway at seventy miles an hour, Zeb took notice that the sky was not just blue, but radiant with greater depth than he had ever witnessed. The pale brown of the sand and dirt seemed to meld into the subtle hues of pink rock, late blooming purple sagebrush and green and gold cactuses. From the corner of his eyes, he caught the action of small animals, lizards and squirrels making sudden darting movements as they scurried toward their destinations. He glanced again toward the azure heavens as the sun, behind the graceful soaring wings of a lone eagle, cast a fleeting shadow across the hood of his car. Omens were everywhere and speaking loudly to him. Perhaps his dream had been real.

17

Zeb found himself passing by the Town Talk Diner. He yearned for a taste of Doreen's sassy banter. A little teasing topped off with a special Tex-Mex burger would be the perfect prelude to asking her to take a little time off work and drive with him out to Antelope Flats to meet with Song Bird. The clock on the dashboard warned him that if he didn't watch the time he would be late for his meeting with the detective.

Through the office window, the sheriff noticed a well-dressed and well-groomed stranger. This guy screamed city slicker with his Italian cut suit, Tony Lama eel-skin boots, Saddleback brief case and Gucci sunglasses resting on the brim of a brand new, store-bought cowboy hat.

The sheriff couldn't help but notice Helen Nazelrod chatting away like a charmed schoolgirl with the broadly smiling young man. Helen, leaning against her desk, was engaged in animated conversation and was no doubt spilling facts and information at the speed of sound. He trusted Helen, but this was his office. He should be controlling the flow of information. This situation he would remedy posthaste.

As the sheriff made an entrance, Helen noted his stern expression and quickly returned to her usual professional demeanor. The change didn't escape the detective.

"Sheriff Zeb Hanks, I presume?"

"You must be Benjamin Jensen. I see you've already met my secretary."

"Yes, lovely woman," said Benjamin. "You're lucky to have her. In Phoenix she could write her own ticket. A woman like her is easily executive secretary material for the best private investigation firm."

Helen blushed radiantly at the compliment.

"She is the best at what she does," said the sheriff dryly. "Step into my office."

The detective quickly detailed Zeb's office with an eyeballing of the room. He scanned over a locked weapons cabinet with its neat display of a dozen rifles and handguns, a photo of a football team from the eighties, a picture of Sheriff Hanks as a detective in Tucson, and some well-worn leather furniture, including a chair too small for a man of the sheriff's stature.

Zeb, in turn, gave the young private cop a quick once over. Outside of the fact that he dressed like he was in the cowboy Mafia, he seemed pleasant enough. His charisma and easy good looks had certainly won Helen over in a hurry.

"What brings you to town?"

Taking a chair opposite the sheriff's desk, Jensen came to the point.

"I need your assistance."

"How so?" asked Sheriff Hanks.

The detective grabbed the leather valise he had placed at his side, raising it to the level of the top of the sheriff's desk. Before placing it on the large desk, he inquired politely.

"May I?"

"By all means."

Sheriff Hanks leaned back and interlocked his fingers behind his head. The detective removed several files and set them on the desk.

"It's a missing persons case," he explained. "One that's turned into quite something else, I suspect."

"What are the particulars on the missing person?" asked the sheriff.

The private detective described a young girl—thirteen years old, ash-blonde hair, five feet two inches tall, blue eyes, one hundred five pounds. He rattled off her social security number, home address and even a list of the extracurricular activities she was involved in at the private Catholic junior high school. Her father was a hotshot criminal lawyer in Phoenix that the detective did a lot of work for. The girl had been missing for a month. Her name was Sara Winchester.

"Sounds like you know who you're looking for," said Zeb. "How'd she end up missing?"

"She's a runaway...maybe. She got into a fight with her old man about the clothes she was wearing, the kids she was hanging out with, the usual. This happened on a Saturday. The next day she leaves home and never comes back."

In Tucson, Zeb had worked on a dozen cases involving runaways. Most of the time they resolved quickly. But a thirteen-year-old girl missing for thirty days certainly wasn't something to be optimistic about.

"What brings you to Safford?"

"I had a lead that puts her at the Flying J truck stop. You know it? It's north of Tucson at the intersection of interstates eight and ten."

"Sure."

"One of the hookers who works the Flying J said she spotted a young girl who matched the description with a creepy looking guy. She described him as a thin, redheaded guy with bad skin who was driving a nineteen sixty-five or sixty-six Mustang. She said the girl looked scared and doped up. When the car drove off, the hooker noticed it had a bumper sticker advertising one of your local establishments, Red's Roadhouse. You know the place?"

"It's just across the county line. It's a shit hole, pig sty frequented by bikers, drunken Indians and about every kind of loser in the five county area. It's populated nightly by trash of every race, creed and color. During the day, it's also a bus stop and a stopping off point for every vagrant passing through the area."

"Other than the fact that it serves a rather classy clientele, what do you know about the place?"

Zeb knew more about Red's than he would ever confess to a private cop. In his misspent youth, he went there often with Maya and Jenny. He could buy beer there because the owner, Red Parrish Senior, had no qualms about selling beer to minors. Even in those crazy days, when Zeb's judgment wasn't so good, his instincts told him the bar and everybody in it was bad news. But Jenny and Maya felt differently about Red's. They loved the seedy joint. It became their hangout. It was also the place where his two good friends went to escape the pressure they felt as daughters of the most highly respected citizens in their individual communities. At Red's Roadhouse they could live outside the tight reins of social mores that inhibited their ability to live the life they thought they wanted to live.

The bar was little more than a black hole to Zeb. He had no doubt it was the influence of Red Parrish Senior and the low-life types that frequented his place that led to Jenny Dablo Bright's long, downhill slide. He also was certain the same alcoholic fate would have met Maya if Jimmy Song Bird had not sent her away to college.

"It's a place where lost souls gather," said the sheriff. "And a place some of them never really leave."

Zeb's response drew a raised eyebrow from the detective.

"What do you know about the current owner?"

"Michael Doerry? He's an odd duck. Calm as the eye of a storm until someone starts asking the wrong questions or starts talking religion."

"And then?"

"He becomes a bull, snorting and scratching in front of a matador's red cape."

"Hates being questioned, huh?"

"He hates, period. Cops are usually the ones asking questions. The way I got it figured they're just convenient scapegoats."

"And religion?"

"I've heard he preaches shit that makes him sound like the anti-Christ. I got him figured for a blowhard. All talk and no action, other than occasionally scaring the pants off a Mormon missionary who stops by to try and spread the word."

"Any idea what makes him tick?"

"Do I look like a psychologist?"

"Did you know Doerry isn't his real name?"

"Nope."

"His real name is Michael Parrish, aka Red Junior."

"That's news to me," replied Zeb.

"I guess his old man owned the place years ago."

"That isn't news to me. I knew Red Senior, but never knew he had a son."

"Did you know Red Junior, aka Michael Doerry, has an arrest record for the sale of child pornography over the Internet?"

"No. I haven't heard anything about that. I wonder how he managed to keep it quiet?"

"Weird privacy laws, that's how."

"How did you find out?"

"Man's best friend, the computer."

"What else don't I know about him?" asked Zeb.

"He served a little time in California for the porno charge. And, get this. While he was in there, he became an ordained minister, mail order variety. Sort of odd for the anti-Christ shit he gets off on, I'd say. When he got out, he laid low and kept his nose clean. After he got off probation, about eighteen months ago, he moved here. That's when Red Junior reopened his old man's bar. Somehow or other the State of Arizona saw fit to give him a license to operate a liquor establishment. I hacked into his business computer. He's still got a thing for the young girls."

Like father like son thought Zeb. Red Parrish Senior had preyed on the underaged Maya and Jenny every time they had set foot in his place. Back in the day old man Parrish's perverted leers at Zeb's close friends made him feel jealous and angry. Though he had no proof, there was a time when Zeb even suspected Jenny's child, Angel, was fathered by Red Senior.

"Did you know the old man?"

"I was pretty young. I knew him more by reputation than personally," said Zeb.

"I heard he disappeared about eight or nine years ago."

"Disappeared? Hardly. The story around here is that he ran off with a teenager," said Zeb. "He had a reputation as being a freak for young girls."

"So the kid learned it from the old man?" asked the detective.

"The fruit never falls far from the tree."

"How do you think he'd take to me having a look around at the bar?"

"He'd make you as trouble in about five seconds flat. Mostly

from that get up you're in. I'd dirty myself up a bit if I was going
to wander up that way. Your duds might work up in Phoenix, but
down here you don't want to wander into the lion's den dressed
like a lamb."

"Thanks for the advice. I need to make something happen.
Time is working against me, and I've got a very powerful father
anxious to see his little girl come home safely. He's pushing
me hard."

"For what it's worth, if I were the missing girl's father, I'd be
more than a little nervous that my daughter was last reported
seen at Red's," warned the sheriff.

"He is extremely nervous," said the detective. "And he's
willing to do just about anything to get his daughter back."

"When you called," said Zeb, "you also wanted to know if I
had a working relationship with the people on the reservation."

"Yes, I did, but I doubt you're going to be able to help me.
Most of the information predates your tenure as sheriff."

"Give it to me anyway."

"I did a search on LexisNexis."

Zeb's puzzled look told the detective he was speaking out of
the sheriff's range of knowledge.

"It's a computer search engine. You can type in a name, for
instance, and pull up all published references to that name. I
typed in Red's Roadhouse and did a search of all newspaper
reports in the state, all arrest records and reports of criminal
activity for the county and state. After that I gained access to all
the tribal police and BIA records for the San Carlos Reservation.
That was no easy task, believe me. When I got all that information, I correlated my findings with a nationwide data bank of
missing persons. I found that over the last twenty years a dozen
missing persons had a direct link to Red's Roadhouse."

"How's that?"

"Either they were known to be heading there, actually seen in the bar or used the bus stop out front. I'm on my way out there now."

Zeb had an uneasy feeling that this case was about to turn a dark corner.

18

Helen Nazelrod was still hard at it an hour past usual working hours.

"Working late tonight, Helen?" asked the sheriff. "Or working ahead?"

"Neither really. I'm just getting a few things in order before tonight's MIA meeting."

Zeb's youth had been filled with endless nights spent at Mutual Improvement Association meetings. He enjoyed socializing with the other teenagers, and the activities were fun. But, seeing those days in retrospect was the real blessing.

"I'm headed for the church. Your paperwork is on your desk," said Helen. "See you in the morning."

Zeb bid his secretary goodnight just as his stomach reverberated with a grinding, mechanical growl. Staring blankly at the paperwork, his gut began to moan like a sick puppy. He patted his stomach like it was a dog's belly. Pushing himself away from the confines of his desk, he addressed the voice inside his abdomen.

"Thanks for the reminder," he said. "I guess it's time to ask

Doreen if she can run up to Wildhorse Canyon and visit Song Bird."

Already his body was sweating in nervous anticipation of asking Doreen to spend the better part of a day with him. The clock on the wall told him the dinner rush hour would be over. In half an hour Doreen would have things put away and in order. He could work a bit longer, then mosey on over to the Town Talk. But the minutes passed too slowly, causing the sheriff to tap the glass cover on his watch to make sure the hands were moving. Outside his window, nothing was moving on the streets of Safford. Everywhere he looked, the world seemed frozen in the moment.

The paperwork lying in front of him bordered on the monotonous, except for a complaint from Mrs. Rajas who had called to report a ghostlike figure hovering in the graveyard. He would stop by later to reassure the nearly blind woman. Odds were nearly one hundred percent that once again, she thought she had seen the ghost of Domingo, her dead husband, wandering among the tombstones. More than once the sheriff had given Mrs. Rajas a ride home after she delivered a plate of tamales to Domingo's grave in the certainty that he was trying to find his way home for dinner.

"He'd never eat any cooking but mine," she would say. "And in heaven they only serve manna, not tamales or tacos. The poor man is probably half starved to death. That's why he wanders out of his grave, you know. He can smell my cooking."

At five minutes to seven, with his stomach aching for Doreen's cooking, Zeb wrapped up his desk work and headed directly to the Town Talk. Taking off his hat, he entered the cafe to the bellowing voice of its owner.

"Hey, trooper," she hollered. "How goes the life of the county's numero uno law dude?"

Zeb glanced around the empty café before taking a seat at

the counter. Everything was spotless and fresh. Salt and pepper shakers, ketchup and mustard bottles were cleaned and full. Napkin holders were bursting at the seams and perfectly placed at the center of the tables. Doreen, bobby pin in mouth, fiddled with her hair. She looked like the proverbial million bucks.

"It was an interesting day, Doreen, a real interesting day. Thank you for asking."

Doreen grinned like a cat spitting canary feathers.

"Well, well, well! An interesting day you say? Is there anything lil' ol' Doe can do to maybe make it a little more than just plain ol' vanilla and mayonnaise interesting?"

Here it was, the end of the day, and Doreen was smiling, happy and full of monkey business. To top it off, the front zipper of her immaculately white waitress uniform exposed a hint more cleavage than usual. Zeb's heart pounded a little faster with the acute awareness the feeling in his gut wasn't just ordinary hunger.

"I guess I'll have the usual, Doreen," he stammered.

"One of these days, Cowboy, you're gonna' order the unusual, and God help me, I just might have a heart attack or, worse, flop face first into a bowl of chili and end up with orange slices in my ears."

Doreen clutched her heart and, spinning with the style and grace of a ballet dancer, pirouetted her way through the kitchen doors. Zeb recognized an angel at play as the sound of her voice echoed against the pots and pans.

"You know something, Zeb?" she said, sticking her head through the serving window. "You might think about hitchin' your wagon to my star. Hell's bell's, just on meals alone, I could save you a pile of dough. Think what you could do with the money you saved."

"Careful what you're fishing for," said Zeb. "You just might get a bite."

Doreen, the kind of woman who knew the difference between trolling and teasing, grabbed a cup of coffee, took a seat on the sheriff's better side and whispered in his ear.

"So, Zeb, why don't you make my day and share some of that so called interestin' stuff with your ever lovin'?"

Zeb's ear felt hot as her breath caressed his lobe.

"I had a special date today."

"You ain't cheatin' on me, are ya', sugar dumplin'?" asked Doreen. "That would about break my heart right in two."

Zeb paused long enough to let her think about what his answer might be.

"No, unless you consider a date with a private detective cheating."

"What's a shamus want with the likes of you? I thought real cops and them fake ones hated each other."

"That's only in the movies and on television."

"TV and movies is real life for most everybody I know," said Doreen.

Doreen leaned with one elbow on the counter, pulled a stashed cigarette from somewhere in her ever-rising, beehive hairdo and waited for Zeb to light it.

"You sound like you don't care much for private cops."

"Don't trust 'em, that's all," replied Doreen.

"Now what did they ever do to you?"

"You tell me why you like 'em, and, if you're reason is good enough, I'll tell you why I don't care for 'em," said Doreen.

The acrimony in the statement rolling off her tongue was as sharp as the four-alarm salsa dripping from his Tex-Mex burger.

"All right, if you insist," said Zeb. "But I bet I can guess."

"Don't change the subject," chided Doreen. "We got a deal. You give me your explanation first."

"Benjamin Jensen is a detective from Phoenix. He's looking for a missing girl, a runaway."

"How old is the girl?" asked Doreen.

"Thirteen."

"That's how old I was when I run away the first time," said Doreen. "Made it all the way from Savannah to Macon. I was trying to make my way up to Washington, DC, to get to my uncle's place. He's a priest, you know. He was the only person who seemed to understand me. I suppose the girl that run away had some big fight with her folks and split, huh?"

"So the story goes."

"Let's see. I bet she was mad because they didn't like her friends, and they wouldn't let her stay out late."

"That's about the size of it," said Zeb. "She been in here talking to you?"

Doreen shook her head side to side. Her expression turned to a remembered sadness.

"That poor little child. She could be in a heap o' trouble. Why'd he think you could help him?"

"He tracked her down, sort of. A hooker from the Flying J, over by eight and ten, may have spotted her in a car with a bumper sticker from Red's Roadhouse."

"That ain't good."

"He thought I might know something about the owner."

"Michael Doerry? He's a real A-number-1 jerk, I'll tell you that for sure. I heard more stories about his little perversions than I care to remember."

Doreen started to get up from the stool next to Zeb. He gently pulled her back down by putting a hand on her shoulder.

"What have you heard?" asked Zeb.

"That freaky-deeky pervert eyes every girl or woman who crosses his path like she's beef on the hoof. You can see it in his eyes that he's lookin' right through your clothes to your nakedness. Don't take no doctor to tell what kind of a sick puppy he is."

"Does he come in here?"

"Not regular like, but he's been in here more than once. I hope he never comes this way again. He makes me real dang nervous."

Doreen reached over and grabbed a half-empty pack of Marlboros from under the counter. With a flick of the finger against the bottom of the pack, she removed a single cigarette. From behind her ear, she grabbed a wooden match and lit it by scraping it against the counter.

"Did he ever accost you?"

"No, but a gal can tell by lookin' that, given half a chance, he'd sure as hell be a heap o' trouble in a hurry."

Doreen got up, walked behind the counter to the deli case and grabbed Zeb a piece of his favorite homemade apple pie. The sweetness of the dessert on his tongue made Zeb momentarily forget about the dead girls, the runaway and Red's Roadhouse.

His private thoughts even went so far as forcing him to stop the fork halfway to his gaping mouth and ask himself, was he falling in love?

"Lost in space, cowboy? Or daydreamin' about the wide open spaces again?"

Doreen placed a light finger on the pulse pumping beneath the crow's feet at the corner of Zeb's eye. Experience had taught her a man's eyes were the windows to his soul. The sheriff's body was speaking loud and clear.

"No," Zeb said clearing his throat. "Just thinking."

Doreen's femininity told her exactly what was roaming around inside Zeb's head. But that same nature demanded that she hear it directly from Zeb's mouth.

"Thinking about what?" she asked.

Drifting in a sea of private thoughts regarding the beautiful woman whose hypnotic voice had just asked him the simplest of questions, Zeb was wondering if the light airiness he felt all around him wasn't another signal that cupid's arrow had struck its mark.

"What?" said Zeb, stalling. "What did you say?"

"What do you mean what? You heard me. I asked you what you were thinking about."

The sight and sound of a man falling in love was something she understood better than the gossip that got parlayed around the café. His answer was evasive, if not a bit disappointing.

"I was thinking," said Zeb. "Would you ride out to Wildhorse Canyon with me in the morning?

"Now that's an unusual request, Zeb. Is it official business or a pleasure trip?"

"It's sort of official business. It could be nice to spend some time together, too," replied Zeb. "But mostly, it's a friendly request from Jimmy Song Bird."

Zeb paused and looked down at his plate sheepishly before saying with all the sincerity he held in his heart.

"And from me, too."

"You're sweet, hon, but it sounds to me like it's got more to do with Amanda Song Bird's murder than it does with me. Go ahead, tell me the truth. You ain't gonna pierce this ol' gals suit of armor quite so easily as all that."

The complexity of his feelings toward Doreen and the need for her cooperation in the case created a conflict of interest. Explaining his dream to her might force him to express his true heart and reveal just how much he cared for her. Plus, there was no telling how Song Bird's interpretation might figure into things.

"It does have to do with Amanda Song Bird's death. But it has to do with a lot of other things too. Things that require more than a little explaining."

Doreen didn't know exactly what he meant, but the look on his face told her it was serious business.

"Well, pardner, what time does the train leave the station?"

"Is nine o'clock too early?"

"I'll be there with bells on, hon'. Ready and waitin'."

The twinkle in Doreen's eye put a lump in Zeb's throat.

"Good, and I'll bring the coffee," replied Zeb. "You bring the sugar."

Leaving twice his normal tip, Zeb said his good-bye and floated out the door. A full moon lit up the night sky. Overhead, the stars were sparkling like the eyes of a woman in love.

Doreen took a quarter from the till and slid it in the jukebox. She punched in E9, her favorite song. The orchestral music filled the empty Town Talk as Rosemary Clooney crooned. Doreen put out the lights, took a chair behind the large street-facing window and gazed at the heavens toward the full moon.

Moonlight and love songs, never out of date. Hearts full of passion, jealousy and hate.

L ittle could she know what filled the hearts of some men.

19

Z eb pulled the freshly washed and vacuumed Dodge Dakota in front of Doreen's house at exactly nine a.m. Parking behind her Harley Davidson, the sheriff removed his hat and checked his appearance in the rearview mirror. He dabbed his fingers against his tongue, picking up just enough moisture to tame a small tuft of unruly hair. A quick sniff to his armpit assured him that his deodorant was effective and no perspiration marks stained his freshly ironed uniform shirt. Giving himself the all systems go, Zeb put the hat back on and stepped out of the truck.

The promise of a new day made him feel like a nervous teenager on a first date. Hands deep in his pants pockets, he ambled toward the front door of Doreen's small house. The brightly painted pink house shimmered in the morning sunlight. Dozens of late blooming asters and azaleas painted a flowerbed that ran the length of the house. Magenta and deep red rose bushes flanked the front door, all of it neatly adorned by a miniature picket fence that demarcated the edge of the perfectly manicured garden.

Doreen came bouncing through the door and down the steps before he had a chance to ring her bell.

"Mornin', pardner," she said. "Just my luck, ain't it?"

"How's that?" asked Zeb.

Doreen pointed toward the sky just over Mount Graham.

"It looks like the good lord above has blessed us with yet another beautiful day."

"Amen," replied Zeb.

"I seen ya' catchin' a gander at my flower beds. You didn't spot any dirty ol' weeds in there, didja?"

"Everything looks perfect to me," said Zeb, his eye trained on Doreen, not the flowers.

It had been months since he had seen her in anything except a waitress uniform. Today she wore a brightly colored dress that clung tightly to the contours of her body. Zeb's mind searched for the correct superlative to describe what he was witnessing. But it was the Apache tear necklace tracing the V of her dress that captured his direct gaze.

"See somethin' you like, darlin?" asked Doreen. "Or just playin' with your imagination?"

Her sassy hint flustered Zeb, sending his tongue into a stumble.

"I, uh, I uh, guess we'd better get going," he mumbled.

Opening the driver's door, Zeb held Doreen's hand as she stepped up into the cab.

"Better watch yourself," said Doreen. "Once a gal gets used to this kind of fancy treatment, she might just be gettin' to believe she's some sorta fairy tale princess."

With the radio preset to WCAW, Doreen's favorite station, they headed up the state highway toward Wildhorse Canyon. The rising sun peaking over the mountaintop to the east shined a soft light on her face. The pure whiteness of her skin, brightened by the morning sunrays gave her a glow of divine innocence. When he drew back to observe her beauty, the front wheels of the truck slipped over the edge of the road, causing the vehicle to swerve.

"Whoa, hold on there, cowboy. Better keep your eyes on the road."

"Whoops," said Zeb. "For a minute I forgot I was in the driver's seat."

"You got something on your mind, or just feelin' a bit scattered this morning?"

Searching for the right words to begin the discussion on exactly why he was taking her on this road trip gave Zeb a severe case of cottonmouth. He licked his lips for a bit of lubrication.

"Jimmy Song Bird," he croaked from a dry throat.

"Hon', I know this trip has something to do with Jimmy Song Bird wanting to talk to me about Amanda. But you haven't told me why he wants to talk to me. Don't you think now is a good time to clue me in?"

Zeb's dry lips stuck together as he began to speak. He swallowed hard a few times.

"It's a story I'm not exactly sure I understand myself," he said.

Doreen cracked the window on the passenger side to allow in some of the desert morning air. Zeb followed suit. Turning his head slightly in Doreen's direction but making certain to keep one eye on the road, he was hypnotized by the unkempt and comely look the wind gave her as it disheveled her hair. Slight touches of make-up, enhanced by daylight on her face, made her look radiantly youthful as the sun danced off her skin. Zeb knew he was looking at the most beautiful woman on the planet. The crosscurrent relaxed him enough to make speech possible.

"I had this dream not too long ago. It was about you."

"About lil' ol' me," said Doreen, bringing her hands over her breast. "Well ain't I the flattered one."

Zeb felt a warm tingling that was destined for his heart launching in the pit of his stomach.

"In my dream you were riding your Harley. I imagined it to be somewhere out on the road past Morenci, where the road straightens out and runs between the mountains."

"I know that spot. I love it there. But as busy as I've been lately, finding the time to ride my hog up that way is only a dream," interrupted Doreen.

"In my dream it was a perfect day. The temperature was perfect, the wind mild and the road didn't have a bump in it. "

"Were you riding with me?" asked Doreen.

"No and yes. I was seeing you, like I was watching a movie, but at the same time I was riding my Harley. Only I wasn't with you."

Doreen snuggled against Zeb's arm.

"If you took the trouble to dream about me, you coulda at least been ridin' with your little pumpkin."

Zeb thought he noticed a hint of disappointment in her voice.

"Sorry. I wish I had been riding with you. You'll see why when I tell you the rest of the story."

"I'm all ears," she said, nuzzling Zeb's shoulder. "Please tell me more."

"I saw that someone was riding on the back of your bike. At first I couldn't make out who it was because your hair was blocking her face. After a moment, the wind moved your hair. It was then I saw your passenger was Amanda Song Bird. Only she was alive and happy."

Once he started talking, the details of his dream flowed from his lips like water from a mountain spring. Doreen watched the wrinkly, smile lines around his eyes smooth out as the tone of his voice became calmer. Each minute detail of his dream seemed to lull her into an almost meditative state. Her utter silence caused Zeb to look her in the eye. Doreen seemed to be staring right through him.

"It was strange..."

In mid-sentence Doreen's voice took over his story.

"...strange," Doreen said, "because I was driving at high speed, through the desert and an eagle was flying alongside me. My passenger giggled in my ear. Her laughing voice was that of a little girl and, at the same time, like what you'd imagine an angel's laughter sounds like. I didn't know who she was. I couldn't turn around to see her. But I knew she was pure. I also knew exactly where I was taking her."

The distant dreaminess of her voice was as stunning as what she said.

"I had the same dream...last night."

Doreen sat up straight in innocent revelation.

"Zeb, can you believe it? We dreamed the same dream."

The soft whir of the wind whispering lazily through the windows said all there was to say. A shared, otherworldly event had passed between them. Zeb, engulfed by a wave of ease, heard only the hypnotic drone of the truck traveling down the road. For a fraction of a second in this strange portal, time ceased its forward momentum.

Doreen, alive with the hum of human electricity, sighed loudly and began to weep softly, joyously. Zeb reached over with his hand and touched her face. Innately, both knew the moment that had just passed between them, with its sweet, graceful fusion of love, was something even more indefinable, a true blessing that would shape their futures. After several moments of sweet silence, Doreen spoke.

"Jimmy Song Bird wants to talk with me about this dream we had?"

"Yes."

"Why? He doesn't know I had it."

"But he knows you were in it."

"Why did you talk to him about the dream?"

"I thought he could tell me what it meant. I don't know why I thought he'd know, I just did. None of my thinking is very logical and rational about what's going on. It's something I feel. Does that make sense to you?"

"Of course it does. Don't forget I'm a woman. What did he say your dream meant?"

"He told me my dream let him know that his granddaughter was free. Song Bird said the dream told him the Great Spirit had come and taken her peacefully to the world of the ancestors. He said the dream removed sadness from his heart. When I told him the dream, he asked if I knew who the woman on the motorcycle was. When I explained that it was you, Song Bird asked if you would come and talk to him."

"Did he tell you what it was he wanted to know from me?"

"Sort of, but not really," said Zeb. "Song Bird was rather vague and mysterious about why he wanted to see you. He would only say he wanted to thank you."

"Thank me? For what?" asked Doreen.

"Uh, I don't really know for sure. I guess I thought that since he's a Medicine Man and you were in the dream with his granddaughter, and in the dream you helped her, I thought that was reason enough to want to thank you. I just assumed it was the Apache way of doing things."

Turning off the main highway onto the side road leading to Wildhorse Canyon, Doreen and Zeb both reached over to roll up the truck windows. The road had been freshly graded, making the ride smoother.

"I've never seen this part of the country," said Doreen. "I thought it was all flat land and scrub desert. I never dreamed there was a place hidden out here that was this lush."

Eskadi Black Robes was standing outside the house when

they arrived. As they stepped out of the truck, the pungent aroma of burning sage drifted over them.

"Eskadi, this is Doreen Nightingale. Doreen, Eskadi Black Robes," said Zeb.

"I recognize you from the café," said Eskadi.

"Didn't I see you in there last week with Deputy Kate Steele?" asked Doreen.

"Please come in the house," beckoned Eskadi, avoiding her question. "Song Bird is fixing you some sassafras tea."

Inside Song Bird's dwelling, the aroma of sage mingled with the sweet smell of mesquite logs crackling in the fireplace. From his seat at the kitchen table, Song Bird rose, moving towards his visitors with the agility of a man half his age. His black hair, speckled with streaks of gray, was pulled into a short ponytail and banded together by a beaded leather strap. Attached to the leather tie was a single eagle feather.

"Song Bird, this is Doreen Nightingale," announced Eskadi.

No sooner had Eskadi spoken than Song Bird reached out with the open palms of his hands inviting Doreen's touch. The graceful manner with which they exchanged a light touch was befitting of royalty. Doreen was overcome with a sense of serenity as Song Bird closed his warm hands around hers and studied the lines on her face. As she looked into his eyes, her heart felt light.

"Walk with me," said Song Bird. "Please."

Doreen mutely obeyed. Walking to the door with her palm rested lightly on the old Apache's ancient fingertips, an airy sensation encompassed her. Song Bird escorted her out of the dwelling, gently placing a hand on Doreen's back. Eskadi and Zeb silently watched the pair as they disappeared beneath the cottonwood and acacia trees into the desert surroundings. Heading down the partially hidden path where Amanda had last been seen, they came quickly within view of Song Bird's daughter's house.

The delightful, harmonious chorale of sounds from the throats of unseen cactus wrens and tree swallows, singing in unison, surrounded them. When they reached the spot on the walkway where Amanda Song Bird was allegedly abducted, a hepatic tanager buzzed just above their heads.

"Your hand on my back feels tremendously hot."

Doreen turned in Song Bird's direction, but as she spoke, her knees buckled. She dropped to the ground, weeping uncontrollably. Through the film of her tears, she saw the apparition of a young Indian girl, running and giggling. The sound of her laughter struck an instant chord. It was the same voice she had heard in her dream. Doreen swooned and her world went dark. She began to shed tears as the vision of the girl became enveloped by a rapidly moving black morass.

Song Bird tenderly wrapped her up in his arms and held her body tightly against his as she wept. When the tears slowed, she spoke involuntarily.

"Perish."

She choked out a single word between deep sets of sobs.

"Perish."

As she spoke, the joyous singing of the birds gave way to an eerie silence. The whole of the natural world stopped as it listened to her words. Doreen's tears pooled in the wizened, wrinkled hands of Song Bird who cradled her head as he sweetly chanted a traditional Apache cleansing prayer.

It could have been a moment or an eternity, but, in Doreen's mind, sorrowful hours passed as Song Bird held her in his arms. When she at last became coherent enough to move, the Medicine Man helped the exhausted Doreen back to his house.

Zeb and Eskadi helped Song Bird lay Doreen on a small bed

in front of the fireplace. Within moments, her tired body was lost to the waking world.

"Is she okay?" asked Zeb. "What's going on?"

"She's fine," assured Song Bird. "There is no need to worry about her. She is exhausted from her ordeal, nothing more."

"What ordeal?"

"I'm certain she will tell you all about it," said Song Bird.

Zeb covered Doreen with a blanket and drew close to her side. Song Bird and Eskadi huddled together momentarily before leaving the house. Together they walked to the ancient mesquite tree where Eskadi helped the old man ceremoniously remove his clothes. Across the sleeping body of Doreen Nightingale, Zeb watched as Eskadi towered over a seated, naked Jimmy Song Bird. Running a cedar branch along the sides of the elder Medicine Man's body, the tribal chairman stopped occasionally, dropping a handful of sand down the wrinkled skin of Song Bird's back. Together the Indians ululated in a haunting, high-pitched tone that made the hair on Zeb's arms stand at attention. Confusion and sadness swept through the sheriff as he watched the men participate in a ritual whose meaning was lost on him.

Four times Eskadi turned away and lay prostrate on the ground as Song Bird changed directions. With each directional rotation, the tribal chairman rose at the Medicine Man's signal and repeated his actions with the cedar branch and sand. When they finished, the old man dressed in new clothes that Eskadi had gathered from the house. Building a small fire, the men burned the shirt and pants Song Bird had been wearing. They left the clothes to burn as the pair paced off slowly in a westerly direction. A moment later they disappeared over the side of a small hill into the dense underbrush.

Zeb sipped sassafras tea and gently rubbed Doreen's back. He thought of Song Bird's loss, of Jake's pain, of Doreen's beauty.

A new sense of compassion was flowing through his veins. He felt afraid, yet free. Afraid of the changes that he knew must come, yet free to choose them. He contemplated what he had just witnessed, wondering if it was all somehow related to the murder of Amanda Song Bird. His new level of this unseen knowledge demanded he understand the connection. In his heart and his head, he couldn't know soon enough.

An hour passed and the sun sat squarely overhead. Sensing that Song Bird and Eskadi would not be returning any time soon, Zeb carried the softly snoring Doreen to the back seat of his truck. Still at a loss to comprehend the morning's events, his intuition hinted that an unseen hand was playing an ever-increasing role in all that was going on around him. He found himself unexpectedly praying for guidance and understanding.

Halfway back to Safford, where the Indian Hot Springs wash ran under the highway, Doreen stirred ever so slightly. Zeb glanced over his shoulder to check on his sleeping beauty. She was purring like a kitten, not moving a solitary muscle. What a different picture she posed, lying there, than when Maya and Jenny would be passed out in the back of his car, drunk.

Zeb saw his life as a circle begun anew as he pulled in front of the pink house and parked once again behind the Harley. Doreen stirred as he shut off the engine of his truck. Moments later she yawned and lifted her weary head, surprised to see they were parked in front of her house.

"Zeb, what are we doing here? Have I been sleeping?"

"You've been out like a light. Don't you remember falling asleep?"

"Not really. The last thing I remember was Song Bird's hand in the middle of my back. I felt very warm, almost hot, and I was certain I was going to faint. Only I didn't. After that, everything just sort of gets hazy."

Doreen rubbed the sleep out of her eyes and let out a burst of laughter.

"I do remember one other thing."

"What was that?"

"I dreamed I was a princess. And you, you were my knight in shining armor carrying me in your arms," said Doreen. "I was trapped and only you could save me from the savages who wanted to make me their slave. You were my hero."

The sheriff's ego soared as he got out of the truck to open the door for his still drowsy passenger. Walking to the house arm in arm with Zeb, Doreen's head suddenly cleared as her eyes fell on the smudged dirt stain on her skirt.

"I fell on the trail," she declared.

"What?" asked Zeb.

Doreen pointed to the dust and dirt just above her knee.

"I just remembered that I fell onto the ground and began crying. It wasn't long after Song Bird and I went for a walk down the trail towards his daughter's house, near where his grand-daughter was kidnapped," she said. "My legs gave way, and I tripped or maybe I collapsed. I don't know for sure. I might have even hit my head and face because my lips feel swollen and numb."

Zeb put a hand on her cheek, allowing his thumb to rest on her lip. She responded with a soft kiss.

"Your lips look fine," he said. "But you say you tripped? What happened? Why did you fall?"

"Song Bird had his hand on the middle of my back. I was listening to the birds singing. It was beautiful, like in a movie or a happy dream. Then, all at once, everything stopped, and the birds quit singing. In that moment of complete silence, I was overcome with so many feelings at the same time that I thought I was going to leap right out of my skin."

Trembling, Doreen put her arms around Zeb and held on tight as she continued her explanation.

"Everything I ever felt about love, hate, joy, happiness and sadness all came shooting through me at once in a big ball of emotion. Let me tell you, that was exhausting. It took the legs right out from under me."

"I can't imagine," said Zeb. "When you walked down there with Song Bird, I knew something important was happening to you. But I didn't know what it was. Tell me, what did Song Bird do?"

"He put his hands on my face and turned my head so I could see directly into his eyes. Instantly I began to dream or at least that's what it felt like. Song Bird's pupils looked way inside of me, and then they turned into eagle's wings. I was scared. I thought I was going to fly. For a split-second I was certain I had gone crazy. Then I fell to the ground in a heap and began to cry. I couldn't control myself. For some reason I kept trying to talk, but only one word came out of my mouth."

"Doe, what word did you say?"

"Perish. I kept saying perish."

"Perish?" asked Zeb, "like...in...to die? Maybe you thought you were dying."

"Maybe, I don't know. I don't think I thought I was going to die. I just know it meant something important. The word perish kept echoing in my ears. Then for a second or two I thought I was going to drown. Imagine that, drowin' in the middle of the desert. Wouldn't that be a weird thing to do? That musta been all those tears I was sheddin'."

Reliving the experience caused Doreen to swoon.

"Zeb, I am so pooped, and I feel lightheaded. I need to lie down. What is going on with me, anyway? I never felt like this before."

In her state of exhaustion and barely able to stand, Zeb lifted

1666166616

her into his arms and carried her in the house. Inside, he lay her on the living room sofa.

"Punkin, would you get me a glass of water?"

Zeb raced into the kitchen, sliding across the newly waxed floor, and poured Doreen a glass of water from the refrigerator. He hurried back to find Doreen barely alert.

"Here, Doe, take a sip."

Holding the glass steadily, he gently poured a teaspoon or two into her mouth.

"I'm so dang tired," she mumbled. "I can barely keep awake."

He wanted to comfort her more but felt so inept. He reached out to hold her as she began to fade. As her lids drifted shut over her deep blue eyes, the rhythm of her breathing slowed its pace to one compatible with sleep. Zeb grabbed the coziest blanket he could find and covered her. Standing back as slumber completely overtook her, Zeb reached down and gently pulled the hair away from her face. He saw only innocence.

Zeb headed to his office. His thoughts drifted back to the events of the morning. Song Bird's mysterious interpretation of his and Doreen's dream, as well as Doreen's reaction, had him stymied.

"Perish? Perish? Perish," he said aloud.

Doreen's intuition had told her it didn't mean to die, but at the same time she felt as though she was going to drown. Perish meant only one thing in Zeb's mind, death. His mind was spinning with that thought as he parked in front of the office.

"Good afternoon, Sheriff. You're looking a little, uh, different today," said Helen.

"Well, I feel a little different today," said Zeb.

Helen extended her hand, which held a neatly folded note.

"I think you're going to want to get to this right away," said Helen. "Your other messages are on your desk."

Sheriff Hanks opened the note. It was a request from Jake

Dablo for a meeting at the Town Talk at three o'clock. That gave him an hour to tend to office matters. Sifting the paperwork on his desk, he remembered back to the days of Sheriff Jake Dablo. Come hell or high water, three o'clock meant it was coffee break time. He shook his head. Jake hadn't been in town for three o'clock coffee in nearly seven years. It was another encouraging sign that Jake might have finally licked the demons that had been chasing him for so long.

"Helen," shouted Zeb, "how did Jake sound when he called?"

"He was real chatty with me. Just like he always used to be in the old days. It sounded like he wanted to talk to you about official business, but I'd say he sounded real good."

Zeb considered the former sheriff's new state of sobriety. In the back of his mind, he hoped that the alcohol washing out of Jake's system had jarred loose some previously known but not comprehended fact about his granddaughter's murder. If the death of Amanda Song Bird was the triggering factor, maybe, just maybe, Jake had a revelation about how the murders were related.

If it were true that Jake's dark days were leaving him, he would have two things on his mind—the murder of Amanda Song Bird and the unresolved death of his granddaughter, Angel Bright. A feeling of hopeful anxiousness ran through Zeb as he made his way to the Town Talk.

20

T he sound of the passing truck startled the killer. He took a deep breath. Realizing he had momentarily nodded off, he quickly brought himself to full attention, chastising himself for making such a stupid mistake. He had parked under some trees behind a big boulder across the road, halfway between Song Bird and his daughter's house. The vehicle was out of sight now, so he didn't know if it was Song Bird, Maya or just someone passing by. He stepped out of the car and cautiously climbed on top of the boulder, making certain not to be seen. Binoculars in hand, he stared down the road. Through the cloud of dust, he could tell it was Song Bird's truck that had passed by.

He scrambled down from the rock and jumped in the car, taking off after the truck. He had been stalking Song Bird, Jake Dablo and Zeb Hanks for months. Only Song Bird carried no pattern to his day. Song Bird was the X factor in his plans. The Medicine Man had too many variables in his life. He could be going somewhere to do a healing or merely on a social call. Wherever he was going, his trail of dust was easy to follow from a distance.

At the highway, the old Indian turned south toward Safford. The killer followed at a safe distance, keeping the truck within view at all times. As he crossed the city limits, he passed by the Wal Mart and the Safeway store. When he passed by the Native American supply store, he knew Song Bird wasn't in town to shop. At the edge of downtown, the stalker watched the truck turn right. One block later it turned left into the parking lot of the Town Talk.

The killer parked across the street in an alley and watched the old Indian step out of his truck and walk into the café. Raising an imaginary gun, he pointed a finger in Song Bird's direction and quietly said, "Bang. You're dead." Then he giggled. His levity came to a halt as he noticed Jake Dablo's beat up old pickup was also parked in the lot along with an official San Carlos Reservation truck. He tapped his fingers against the wheel and checked the time. Three o'clock. What were Jake and Eskadi doing there? It wasn't something in either of their routines. His head snapped suddenly to the left as a kid on a bicycle shot by his car door. Take it easy, he reminded himself. Turn lemons into lemonade. Learn something.

He pulled his binoculars from the glove compartment. The shadows and the sun glare on the café windows made it impossible for him to see inside. He would have to get out of his car and walk down the street in broad daylight if he was going to see what was going on. His heart beat a little faster, not much, just enough to notice. He liked the feeling of danger.

He pulled the car out of the alley and across the street, parking behind a semi-truck for cover. He stepped out of the car, leaving the door unlocked. He slipped on a pair of sunglasses. Even now, in late autumn, the sun felt hot, too hot. He preferred the coolness of night.

Staying close to the buildings, under the awnings in the shaded recesses of the sidewalk, he walked casually toward the

Town Talk. Two old women passed him. He was pleased as they all mutually ignored each other.

He passed the entrance to the café and ambled slowly past the large glass windows in front of the building. Glancing into the café as he moved by, he noticed little because of the sun and shadows. He continued on to the end of the block and stopped, bending over to tie a shoelace that had not come undone. He needed a plan. He reminded himself to think clearly.

Reversing his tracks, he made a second pass at the café, this time stopping in front of an advertisement for the county fair placed in the window. Now he could see clearly into the restaurant. It took him only a moment to realize he was watching a meeting with Song Bird, Jake Dablo, and Eskadi Black Robes.

He turned to spit, but stopped when his eye caught the reflection of a tall man in a cowboy hat walking toward the café entrance. The killer brought his hand to his cheek and rubbed the corner of his eye in an attempt to cover his face.

Sheriff Hanks was the fourth man at this meeting.

21

Hanging his cowboy hat on the antler rack, Zeb glanced around the room. The café was bustling with men on midday break. At one table businessmen animatedly discussed the current state of the local economy. At another, farmers ranted and raved about cotton and cattle prices as well as the failure of the Department of Agriculture to prop up price supports as they had promised they would. There was more than a little talk of throwing the bums out of office on Election Day. At one of the back tables, hidden behind a small wall, a cross section of retired guys played liars poker. The sheriff exchanged nods and howdies with each group.

Zeb noticed Jake, at the counter laughing and shaking dice with Eskadi Black Robes. They were gabbing away like long lost friends. Behind the counter, Maxine Miller was hustling away, keeping things running as smoothly as she could without the aid of the napping Doreen.

"Sheriff, have a seat," said Jake. "We're rolling for coffee. If you lose, we're shaking for coffee and sweet rolls."

Jake and Eskadi broke into the laughter of those involved in an inside joke.

"Here." Jake handed the dice cup to the sheriff.

Zeb took the cup reluctantly, double-checking to make certain they hadn't short diced him. A pair of deuces with his first toss brought even more uproarious laughter from Eskadi and Jake. Assuming he'd been set up, Zeb looked suspiciously at his counter mates.

"Dice are working against me today?" he said.

"I put an ancient Apache curse on them," said Eskadi.

"Maxine," called Jake, "sweet rolls for everyone, and make it a pair for me. I brought a real nasty sweet tooth to town with me this afternoon."

With a sweep of her small arm, Maxine gestured around the entire restaurant.

"Everyone?" she asked meekly. "Are you sure?"

"Heavens yes, everyone," bellowed Jake. "You don't want the people of our fair city thinking that Sheriff Zebulon Josiah Hanks is some kind of a skinflint, do you?"

Zeb dug deeply into his pants pocket for folding money as he took a seat. Slapping the cash on the counter, his eyes caught a glimpse of an image on the mirrored back wall. Staring back at him was the face of Jimmy Song Bird.

"Hon Dah," said Song Bird.

"Jimmy, Jimmy Song Bird," said Zeb. "I didn't see you when I came in. I'm glad you're here."

"I was watching some old men play liars poker."

"I know this is a terrible time, but it's damn good to see you face to face. Thanks for coming."

The gathering of Song Bird, Eskadi Black Robes, Zeb Hanks and Jake Dablo, strong men representing opposing cultures and different eras, made for an unusual sight in the café.

"Let's get down to business and lay all of our cards on the table," said Jake, pushing aside the dice cup. "What each of us knows separately, and what each of us surmises on our own, won't get us anywhere. Our strength will come from combining our knowledge. There's an adage that tells us the whole is greater than the sum of its parts. Look around, gentlemen. That old saying describes our little group perfectly. We have no choice but to work as one, united team." Jake rested his hand on Eskadi's shoulder and squeezed down hard. "That means all of us."

Eskadi winced, but held the same look of determination in his eyes that the other men did.

"It's no secret that I've parked my sorry ass in the bottom a whiskey barrel for almost seven years. Seven years," Jake sighed. "That's a lifetime for some. For years I believed the death of my precious granddaughter, Angel, was the reason for my being a low-life, cowardly drunkard. But I had it all wrong. The truth is I damn near killed myself by wallowing in hatred. Self-hatred, hatred of others, hatred of everything that got to live and breathe while my granddaughter lay cold in her grave. That resentment injured my spirit and darkened my soul. If I hadn't been so self-centered, justice may have been served for my little Angel a long time ago. But now something has changed. My spirit has chosen to quit destroying itself. The wounds in my heart are healing."

Moved by Jake's confession, the men offered silent prayers of thanks to God and the Great Spirit. Zeb suspected Song Bird somehow had a hand in helping Jake transform his long standing personal grief into a healing.

"We have some solid facts," continued Jake. "We know both killings took place on the eighteenth of October. Why the date is significant we don't know. We need to find out what relationship it has to the murders. We know both the bodies were discovered with burning candles placed around them at each of the four directions, with a fifth candle being placed above the head."

"A pentagram," said Eskadi. "Traditional sign of evil."

"Both were preparing for a traditional ceremony, Angel for baptism into the Church of Jesus Christ of Latter Day Saints and Song Bird's granddaughter for initiation in the Apache tribe with the Sunrise Ceremony. Each child was dressed in clothing related to her ceremony. Lastly, we know that both these innocents were mutilated. Their hearts were removed from their chests and replaced with religious objects. This information doesn't prove it, but the facts point to a very high likelihood the same person was responsible for both crimes."

The men sat quietly, digesting what they had just heard. Song Bird broke the silence.

"The injured spirit of the killer has come to me in a vision," said the Medicine Man. "He kills children because he walks every day with the pain and loss of abandonment he suffered. We can help him only by stopping him before he kills again. It is our duty. It is our obligation as men."

"I'm certain the killer has left evidence behind that we haven't found," said Zeb. "We need to find it. We need to go back to the beginning and rethink what we already know."

Zeb knew his command would be difficult on the men who had lost their granddaughters. The sheriff well understood what he was asking of Song Bird and Jake. Both men would be forced to relive the past and stare their personal angst in the face. The emotional pain that would be stirred up by talking about the horrific details surrounding the end of their granddaughters' lives was more than he should ask of any man. But there was no other option.

Song Bird brought the deep, dark coffee to his lips. Jake slowly stirred sugar into his swirling black liquid. Neither man broke direct eye contact with Zeb. Yet both men appeared to be looking inward.

"I think one key fact is knowing that both children were murdered as they were preparing for a rite of passage. These rites are similar in that they mark passage into a state of religious and cultural maturity."

"The Sunrise Ceremony is about triumph over the dark forces of nature, both personally and in a larger sense. It's about becoming a woman. Like a Mormon baptism, it purifies the soul and creates a link with God," interjected Song Bird.

"The killer, if it is the same person, obviously wanted to be certain his victims didn't achieve this mature link with God. That may be why he killed them both on the cusp of their reconnection with the spirit," added Jake.

"Maybe he hates the Apache culture," suggested Eskadi.

"Or the Mormon religion," said Zeb.

"Or children," said Jake.

"Or women," added Zeb.

"His hatred is of himself," said Song Bird.

Song Bird's words brought silence to the table. It was becoming clear to all of them the nature of their common enemy was pure evil.

"Removal of the heart?" asked Zeb. "What purpose does it serve?"

"Perhaps he used their hearts in a religious ceremony of his own," said Eskadi.

"And maybe he's just a madman who gets his kicks dissecting the human body," added Jake.

"My vision has spoken to me about such matters," said Song Bird. "The man with the injured spirit believes the heart is the vessel for the soul. With his actions, he seeks to redeem himself and those in his circle."

"I will use everything in my power, including everything said here today, to find the killer. But what I really need is some new, hard evidence," said Zeb.

"Then I have something for you," said Jake. "He took something from our Angel besides her life. He stole a cameo necklace she was wearing."

"I've read the police reports cover to cover a dozen times. That was never reported. Not even the local gossipmongers have brought it up," said Zeb. "Are you certain?"

"No one could have spoken of it. My wife gave her the cameo. It was a private, personal gift passed between generations of women. About three years after Angel died, my wife, ex-wife by then, and I were talking about better days. The immediate hurt of Angel's death had passed, and my wife was seeing a counselor who advised her to talk with me about our granddaughter's death. It was then she told me about the cameo necklace she'd given Angel the day before her murder. It was never found. She was so broken up when her little Angel died that she couldn't bring herself to look at the body during the viewing. She assumed the necklace was buried with Angel. The funeral director's records and my recollection were the same. There was no necklace around her neck. It turned out to be missing, but, at the time of the murder, no one even knew to look for it. Like I said, we didn't even figure it out until three years later. It's been gnawing at the back of my mind ever since, but I never knew what to do with the information."

Song Bird cleared his throat when Jake finished. As he spoke, his words cut like a knife.

"When my daughter, Maya, performed her Sunrise Ceremony, my wife gave her a necklace of lapis and gold. It was the one her mother made for her and her grandmother made for her mother. In Apache tradition, this ornament along with a second, new one made by the mother, is then handed down. Maya gave the traditional necklace to her daughter, my granddaughter, as she was preparing for her sacred ceremony. This necklace is also missing. Zeb you saw the second one at my house."

A common thought ran through the men's heads. If one or both of the necklaces could be found, they could represent the vital clues needed to help break the case.

"I believe more answers might be found within Zeb's dream," said Song Bird.

The sheriff hesitated momentarily and took a deep breath. He felt calmness come over him as he looked deeply into Song Bird's eyes. The other men remained silent as Zeb told his dream-story of Doreen driving the Harley Davidson, Amanda Song Bird her passenger, laughing, hair flying in the breeze. He slowly retold the details of the joy Amanda exuded, the eagle flying alongside the motorcycle, and the image he envisioned in the clouds. With each retelling, Zeb's memory of the dream became more vivid. But this time it dawned on him that he had seen the necklaces the men were describing.

"In my dream, I saw a cameo necklace around Angel's neck and a lapis and gold necklace around Amanda's. Doreen had the identical dream and saw the same thing," said Zeb.

Utter stillness followed his confession.

"The dream tells me my granddaughter is safe," said Song Bird. "She lives in the other world with the ancestors of our people. The eagle and the sky spirits have also told me my granddaughter didn't leave for the world of the ancestors until she passed on information to Doreen. That knowledge will help us find the murderer."

Maxine came by with the coffeepot and asked shyly.

"More coffee?"

Her question eased some of the tension from the air. The men smiled as they pushed their empty cups in her direction. As she poured fresh coffee for everyone, Song Bird continued.

"Doreen came to visit me. We walked near the place where my granddaughter was taken, and my granddaughter's purified spirit uttered one word through Doreen's mouth. The word was 'perish'. Perish!"

Maxine put her hand over her mouth and gasped. The four men's heads collectively rotated as the glass coffee urn fell from her hand and exploded against the linoleum. Everyone in the restaurant turned to see what the commotion was.

"Oh, I'm sorry, so sorry," stammered Maxine.

Embarrassed and scrambling to pick up the remains of the broken pot, the waitress begged their forgiveness.

"It just slipped out of my hand. I, I don't know what happened. I'm sorry. I'm so sorry! Is everyone alright? Did anyone get burned? It's such a mess."

"It's all right, Maxine, it's okay."

The comforting words of Sheriff Hanks, who knelt to help her pick up the mess, did little to calm the young woman.

"I'll get something to clean it right away."

The flustered waitress ran off to get a mop just as tears began to roll down her cheeks. When she returned, Jake, who hadn't spoken a single word during the entire incident, placed a gently reassuring hand on Maxine's shoulder.

"Are you okay?" he asked.

"Yes, I'm fine."

"Well, Maxine, don't worry about what just happened. These kinds of things are just simple mistakes. Everybody makes them. I've made a few myself, quite a few as a matter of fact."

The gentle words from the older man failed to reassure her, and she ran sobbing into the kitchen. Failing to understand, the four men returned to their previous conversation.

"We're going to have to trust each other," said Zeb. "And share everything we learn. Eskadi, you nose around out on the reservation. See what you can find. Song Bird, if you think of anything else, let me know right away. Anyone have anything else they'd like to add?"

"When do we meet again?" asked Eskadi.

"Tomorrow," said Zeb. "We'll need to put our heads together and formulate a precise plan of action. Good luck, men."

Eskadi and Song Bird got up to leave. Jake stayed on for another coffee refill. Zeb hung around hoping Doreen would pop in. But even before he had the chance to see her, he heard Doreen's sweet voice consoling the distraught Maxine.

"Honest, hon', it's okay. It was an old thing anyway," she said. "Don't you worry your purty lil' head over such a thing."

Doreen's kindness struck an invisible chord, causing Maxine to break into heartfelt sobbing.

"Hold on there, kiddo. It's all right. Now what's the matter, really? You can't be that shook up over a little busted up plastic and glass," said Doreen.

Maxine's tears became a river of distress and pain. Jake and Zeb, listening in on all the commotion, peered into the kitchen, curious to know exactly what the problem really was.

"I thought I'd put it all behind me," bawled Maxine. "I didn't think that just hearing his name would set me off. I'm so sorry."

As the young woman continued to weep uncontrollably, Doreen held Maxine in a motherly embrace. Gradually, Maxine began to regain her composure. Still being rocked in Doreen's arms, she wiped her tears away with a dishtowel.

"Who is *he*? Whose name set you off like that, hon'?" asked Doreen.

"Parrish, Mike Parrish. The one they call Red Junior."

Doreen, more concerned about Maxine's emotional state, let the name of Michael Parrish go in one ear and out of the other. But the name wasn't lost on Jake and Zeb. Doreen dabbed Maxine's eyes with a Kleenex and straightened her messy hair.

"Mike Parrish," repeated Maxine.

The sniffles began anew and quickly turned to a torrent of tears as Maxine once again said the man's name.

"Did you say Parrish?" asked a startled Doreen.

Jake and Zeb's hearts raced in unison with the realization this could be just the break they had been waiting for. Could the word 'perish' Doreen had uttered when she collapsed on the ground out at Song Bird's house be Parrish, as in Michael Parrish? Was this the mystical, missing link they had all been praying for?

"Let's sit down and have something to drink," said Doreen.

As the ladies came through the kitchen door, Doreen signaled Jake and Zeb with her eyes to have a seat in the adjoining booth. She knew they had overheard Maxine's outburst and well understood they would have a few questions of their own.

"Mike Parrish?" whispered Zeb. "Red Parrish Junior?"

"I knew his old man. Red Senior. He was a real bastard," replied Jake.

"I remember Red Senior," said Zeb. "I heard he just disappeared one day. Is that right?"

Jake turned to Zeb and gave him a look quite unlike one Zeb had ever seen in his former mentor's eyes. It was a hard, secretive, faraway look, part hatred, part fear.

"Word is he ran off with some teenager he was banging," said Jake. "It all happened when you were away."

"I haven't proven it yet, but I've got it on pretty good authority that Red Parrish Junior is back in town," said Zeb. "Only he's calling himself Michael Doerry. If it's true, he could be the Parrish in Doreen's vision and the one we're looking for."

Doreen and Maxine continued chatting woman to woman in the adjoining booth.

"I think the sheriff has a few things he might like to talk to you about," Doreen said.

"I didn't spill coffee on his uniform, did I?" asked Maxine.

"No. No, it's nothing like that."

"Well what then, I haven't broken any laws, have I?"

"No, not that I know of," laughed Doreen. "I think it has to do with Mike Parrish."

Maxine's eyes couldn't hide behind the glaze of dejection. "Oh."

Doreen nodded at Zeb. He recognized it as the okay signal to approach the table. Maxine looked up at him, trying with all her earthly might to fight back tears.

"Do you mind if we sit down and join you?" asked Zeb. "We have a couple of simple questions for you."

"Have a seat, Sheriff," said Maxine. "I'm so sorry about the coffee. It just slipped out of my hands."

"It's okay. No harm done. Except to the pot."

The sheriff's feeble attempt at humor was met with a cold silence. Eskadi Black Robes, who had returned to the café to pick up his car keys, stood in the background, listening in on the conversation.

"I would like to ask you about Mike Parrish, the one they call Red Junior."

Maxine avoided eye contact with the questioning sheriff.

"I suppose," she replied. "If you insist."

"How do you know him?"

"From high school, mostly, I guess. He asked me out on a date a few times," said Maxine.

"Did you go out with him?"

"Once, sort of. You see it was my senior year, and I had never been asked out on a date. I thought I was going to graduate and turn into an old maid. Looking back, I was naïve and desperate. That's why I said yes. I never really liked him. In fact, I always thought he was a real creep. Turns out I was right," said Maxine, bursting into a hard cry.

Doreen hugged the sobbing waitress and wiped away her tears.

"Are you okay, honey? You don't have to talk about all this right now if you don't want to," said Doreen.

"It's okay. It feels terrible to have it brought up again. But, at the same time, it feels good too. Sheriff, you asked me what happened. Well, I'll tell you exactly what happened. Mike took me out on a date. When he picked me up, he brought me flowers. I thought that was so sweet. We went swimming out at Ropers Lake. We were having fun, or so I thought, when suddenly he yanked off the upper half of my swimming suit and ran on shore. He stood there laughing like crazy, whipping my top in circles over his head. I begged him to throw it back to me but he wouldn't. At first I was embarrassed. Then he ran to his car and got a camera. He said he was going to take my picture when I came out of the water. I stayed in the lake as long as I could, but finally I just got too cold. I tried to sneak out and grab my towel, but he knocked me down and forced himself on top of me. I was really scared. Just then a car drove by, and I screamed as loud as I could. He let loose of his grip on me for a second and I escaped. I know he would have raped me if I hadn't gotten away."

The redness in Maxine's eyes and face disappeared as she unloaded her long-shouldered burden. She took a sip of her iced tea and addressed the sheriff tersely.

"Now I know I should have reported him for assault or attempted rape or something like that. But at the time I didn't have enough confidence in myself to think anyone would believe me. And everyone knows the cops never believe the victim anyway."

"I know this is upsetting," said Zeb. "But do you mind answering a few more questions. It could be very important."

"I don't mind."

"Did he ever mistreat you after that?"

"He called me the next day and told me he'd kill me if I ever told anyone what happened. He said he had a gun and would shoot me. He told me I'd never even see it coming. I figured it was just crazy talk to keep me from talking about the attack. I never really thought he'd do it. I never talked to him after that, but it was right about that time that his dad ran off. Since his mom and dad were divorced, Michael moved away to live with her. Good riddance to bad rubbish is what I say."

"It's terrible that you ever had to go through anything like that, hon'. Things like that shouldn't happen to no one," said Doreen.

"You know something," said Maxine. "I had put it way out of my mind. I hadn't even thought about it for years, until today when you said his name."

"Were you aware that Michael Parrish moved back to the area?" asked Zeb.

A look of horror came over Maxine's face.

"No, no, no," she shrieked

"Take it easy," said Zeb. "He's not going to hurt you. We'll see to that."

"You can't," cried Maxine. "You don't understand. You can't protect me from him. He's evil."

22

Zeb and Jake headed for the sheriff's office. As Zeb held the office door open for Jake he glanced down the street and noticed Eskadi's truck parked nearby. Jake headed directly to Helen's desk with a pair of blueberry muffins.

"Helen, let me have a look at you. You are a sight for sore eyes," said Jake.

The normally reserved secretary scooted out from behind her desk, threw her arms around her former boss and gave him a big bear hug. After a moment, she stepped back, eyed him up and down and sighed deeply before embracing him a second time.

There was no mistaking the alcohol-induced, spider-web pattern of broken blood vessels around Jake's nose. But the wrinkles in his weathered skin smoothed as he grinned, and the smile lines at the corners of his eyes revealed the same old handsome countenance. Jake Dablo still carried the unmistakable, magical spark of a true western man.

"Jake, I've been praying for this day for a long time," said Helen.

"Well don't quit your praying now. I can still use the help. Damn likely more than ever."

Jake and Helen separated from the embrace, stood back and looked at each other in a way that only old, trusting friends can.

"Enough of the mutual admiration society," said Zeb. "We're still running a sheriff's office here, aren't we?"

"Oh, yes. I nearly forgot," said Helen. "Mr. Jimmy Song Bird and Mr. Eskadi Black Robes are waiting for you in your office. They said you would be expecting them and you told them to wait in your office."

In the sheriff's private office, the tribal chairman and the Medicine Man stood by the window.

"What have you found out about Michael Parrish?" asked Song Bird.

Having not seen Eskadi re-enter the restaurant, Zeb looked at the Medicine Man wondering if like Big Bear, the ancient Apache from his youth, he possessed some sort of second sight.

Zeb gave the details of what he'd learned about Michael Parrish. The buzzing of the intercom interrupted him.

"Yes, Helen," said the sheriff, "what is it?"

"Detective Jensen is here. He wants to talk with you."

"Tell him to wait."

"He says it's very important and, considering what you're talking about..."

Sheriff Hanks eyed the slightly ajar door. Helen's ears must have been on fire.

"What's he want?"

"It's about Michael Doerry, aka Red Parrish Junior. He's been standing out here right beside me nearly the whole time you've been talking. He's heard every word you said."

"Send him in."

The private detective's swollen left eye and bloodied shirt spoke for him.

"What the hell happened to you?" asked Zeb.

"Red Parrish must have thought I was a Mormon missionary."

Eskadi's chuckle broke the tension. The sheriff introduced everyone.

"I heard what you were saying about Red Parrish, Senior. But you're wrong about one thing. He didn't run away. He's dead," said Jensen.

"Red Junior tell you that?" asked Zeb.

"Not exactly."

Private Investigator Jensen reached into his pocket and pulled out a Polaroid of a headstone. Zeb examined it briefly before handing it to Jake. Jake glanced at it and handed it back to Zeb.

"Where'd you get this?" asked Jake.

"Junior had it on his desk in that office he keeps behind the Roadhouse."

"He let you in there to look around?" asked Zeb.

"The door was open, so I let myself in," said the detective. "I knocked first."

"See anything else of interest?"

"I didn't have a whole lot of time before I had company. All I noticed was a bunch of old mattresses stacked up in a corner."

Red's mattress factory, thought Zeb. Hookers rented the beds for five bucks a pop when they took their johns from the bar to the shed.

"There were some miscellaneous papers, some file cabinets and a box full of child pornography magazines."

"That sick bastard," growled Zeb. "Anything else in sight?"

"An old car in pretty good shape, except for a busted taillight and a slightly bent frame. It was a Ford Mustang."

Zeb looked at the Antelope Flats file case that sat on his desk. Next to it was the piece of colored plastic he had found on the road near where Amanda Song Bird had been kidnapped. Zeb slipped the small piece into his shirt pocket.

"What bought you the bloody nose and the shiner?" asked Jake.

"Strictly my fault. He thought I was trespassing. An honest mistake. Any of you know where this head stone might be located?" asked the detective.

A shocked expression came over Zeb's face as he examined the photo closely.

"Hell yes," said Zeb. "It's the Veteran's Memorial Cemetery in Morenci. I recognize the War Memorial in the distant background. But there's something even more interesting than the fact that it's Red Senior's grave. Jake, Song Bird, take a look at the death date."

Both men put on their glasses, scrunched up their noses and squinted at the small photo. October 18, 1991. No one said a word until Jake stood up and excused himself.

"Where are you headed, Jake?"

"To the grave of Red Parrish. To find some answers," he said. "Maybe the dead man will speak to me."

"Hold on," said Zeb. "We're all going with you."

Song Bird sat in the front seat of Jake's truck, Eskadi and Zeb hopped in the back. The detective followed solo in his car. Inside the west entrance of the cemetery, next to a grave marked by a statue of the Sacred Heart of Jesus, the men parked and fanned out in search of the final resting place of Red Parrish.

"Over here," shouted Zeb.

Five rows from the back, near the south end of the cemetery, lay the remains of Robert Parrish. The men gathered around the granite marker that read:

ROBERT HORATIO PARRISH
'RED'

Born January 21, 1941—Died October 18, 1991
Devoted Father

Sheriff Hanks stared at the gravestone. Song Bird and Jake
exchanged a hard, meaningful glance.

"October eighteenth," said Zeb. "October eighteenth."

The men all stared at the marker.

Song Bird knelt on both knees near the grave of Robert
Parrish. Thinking the Medicine Man was about to pray, Zeb
bowed his head to join him. Zeb's eyes, half-squinted shut in
prayer, eyed Song Bird as he leaned forward and put his hands
into a patch of desert grass near the marker.

The sheriff's eyes opened wide when Song Bird, digging in
the soil with his bare hands, pulled out something that glittered
just beneath the surface. The Medicine Man's lower lip quivered
involuntarily as he held the shining object over his heart. A full
five minutes passed before anyone moved. Song Bird stood
slowly, clutching the item in his hand.

"This was the sacred traditional family gift that was given to
my granddaughter."

Song Bird held the necklace in the air.

"When it was given to my granddaughter, she said she would
never take it off. She was wearing it when she was killed. Only
the murderer could have carried it to this spot."

His statement penetrated the other men as only the truth
can. Jake Dablo turned abruptly, walked back to his car, opened
the trunk and removed a metal detector. Toying with the adjust-
ment knobs, he walked back towards the graves where he
methodically ran the guide plate around the edges of the grave
of Robert Parrish. When no response registered on the
machine's readout meter, he covered the same territory again,

this time holding it directly against the rim of the tombstone. The indicator siren screeched loudly this time. Leaning the metal detector against an adjoining grave, Jake bent over and began to carefully remove the sand, dirt and grass with a pocketknife. Moments later, he pulled something from the soil, a small locket. Inside was the photo of a young girl, not older than twelve or thirteen. Jake rubbed the dirt and sand off the glass covering and handed it to the detective.

"Is this the girl you're looking for?"

Investigator Jensen examined it in the bright of the sunshine and then handed it to Sheriff Hanks.

"Yes," he said. "I'm afraid it is."

"I'm afraid our killer may have struck again," said Zeb.

"There's something else you should know," said Jensen. "The man buried in that grave, Red Parrish, had a professional relationship with my client."

"How's that?" asked the sheriff.

"I suppose I should have told you earlier. My client defended Red against a rape charge in Phoenix about twenty-five years ago. He lost the case, and Red did five years in the state pen. When he got out, he made continual threats against my client's family. But since he's six feet under, he isn't much of a suspect."

"Which points the finger directly at his son," said Jake.

"Wait a second," said Zeb. "How do we know Red is actually buried here? After all, he was reported missing, not dead. It wouldn't take ten minutes to make a phone call and see if there's an official certificate of death. I'll call Helen on the two-way and have her call the state. She might even be able to look up official death records on the computer."

Fifteen minutes passed before Helen called to inform them there was no official record of Red Parrish Senior's death with either the state or the Social Security Administration.

"The cemetery must have a manager or an overseer," said

Zeb. "He'd have a record of when the headstone was placed here."

A secretary at city hall directed them to Ivan Goetz. The old man appeared befuddled when the five men knocked on his door until they explained what they were looking for.

"Nope, ain't no body in that grave. Just a memorial marker," he said.

"How long has it been there?" asked the sheriff.

The old man scratched his thinning, white hair and spit a slag of slimy tobacco on the ground.

"About a year. Maybe a bit more. I can look it up if you need an exact date. Why do you want to know? Is this official business?"

"Yes, it is," said the sheriff. "Do you know who had the marker put there?"

"His kid, I believe. He was a nasty fella with a tuft of red hair that stuck straight up like a banty rooster. Ornery young man. A real punk."

"Did you have a run in with him?" asked Jake.

"More than once," the man replied, taking the opportunity to spit some more chaw on the ground.

"Recently, by any chance?" asked Zeb.

"Sure enough. Just yesterday as a matter of fact. He was kneelin' by the marker, prayin' it looked like. I took off my hat, respectful like, and waited 'til he was done. When he stood up, I went on over and asked him if the site looked okay or if he needed something special done. I was just doin' my job. He told me to get the hell away and to stay away from his old man's marker. Usually folks are pretty nice when they're visitin' the dead ones. But not him. He done somethin'?"

"He might have," said Zeb.

"You want me to give you a call if he shows up again?"

Zeb handed the man his business card. The old man stared at it.

"He might have killed someone. Be careful around him. We consider him to be armed and dangerous."

"I can handle myself. I own a dozen guns. I fought in the big one at Iwo Jima. I ain't about to take no crap from some young whippersnapper."

"Please just call me," said the sheriff. "Don't confront him."

The old man hurtled a chaw of tobacco spit near the sheriff's foot.

"Bah. Country's goin' to hell in a hand basket. The good guys can't even take care of the bad ones no more without gettin' in a heap of trouble. It's a damn shame, is what it is. I can take care of myself and that little bastard."

The old man hurled one final spit of tobacco juice and slammed the door.

"Sheriff, you think Red Senior is dead?" asked the detective. "Or alive and seeking revenge on those who have wronged him?"

Song Bird and Jake remained mute and emotionless.

"I know old man Parrish knew both Jenny and Maya," said Zeb. "From what the detective tells us, he also had a direct link with his client and he'd threatened him. If Red is alive and kidnapped Attorney Winchester's daughter, it gives us a pretty clear indication of his modus operandi."

"What do you mean?" asked Eskadi.

"If Red had a vendetta against the attorney and kidnapped his daughter, maybe he also had a vendetta against Maya and Jenny and took it out on their kids."

"Or maybe he had an old score to settle with Jake and Song Bird," said Eskadi. "Jake, you said you knew Red. What about it?"

Jake's only response was the exchange of a dour, grim glance with Song Bird.

23

"Sheriff, my client's daughter is still missing," said the detective. "There has got to be enough circumstantial evidence for you to go up there and have a look. With his record, isn't the presence of child porn magazines good enough reason to investigate further?"

"You'll need a search warrant," said Jake. "Otherwise, anything you find could get suppressed as evidence if this thing ever goes to trial."

"How about it, Sheriff?" asked the detective. "There's still a small chance Sara Winchester could be alive."

"It will take me a couple of hours to get a hold of Judge Frank. I'll have to disrupt his day and convince him of the necessity for a search."

"Sara Winchester's life might depend on it," said the detective. "The last thing this county needs is another dead child on its hands."

"Eskadi," said Zeb. "I'm going to have to ask you to leave."

"Why?" asked Eskadi.

"Things might get a little rough. The Parrish Family is known for violence. I can't risk a civilian getting hurt."

"I can take care of myself," replied Eskadi.

"I know you can," said Zeb. "But this is not the place for you to be. End of discussion."

More than once over the years, the sheriff and tribal chief had not seen eye to eye. This time, something told Eskadi that Zeb had something other than Eskadi's safety on his mind. This was not reservation turf and not his business.

"Okay. I guess I'm out of here," said Eskadi. "But if you end up one man short, don't come crying to me."

Jake chuckled at that.

"Don't worry, we won't," replied Zeb.

Two hours later Sheriff Hanks, Deputy Kate Steele and Benjamin Jensen knocked loudly on the locked front door of Red's Roadhouse. When no one answered, they made their way behind the Roadhouse to the shed that doubled as an office and whorehouse. It was unlocked.

Zeb was familiar with the layout of the building from his younger days. His eyes fell on the stack of moldy mattresses. It was on one of those mattresses that Zeb had given up his virginity to Jenny Dablo. At the time, it was scary and exciting. But now, in the dingy, run-down shed, he felt ashamed.

"Here's the car I was telling you about," said the detective. "Sixty-five Mustang Pony, bent frame, busted taillight."

Zeb stuck his head in the open window of the car. Sitting on the passenger's seat floor was a green Coleman cooler. Zeb started to walk around the car to have a look at the broken tail light. He pulled the fragment of plastic from his pocket and held it against the back of the car. It was a perfect match.

"Sheriff Hanks," said Jensen. "Look at this."

The private detective stood near the open drawer of a storage cabinet that was jammed with wallets, wristwatches, rings and stacks of pornographic magazines.

"The driver's licenses and IDs are all Native American," he said. "All of them from the San Carlos Reservation."

"Sheriff," shouted Deputy Steele. "I've got something over here you're going to want to have a look at."

The deputy held a leather doctor's bag in her hands. The sheriff shined a flashlight inside the bag. A pair of latex gloves covered a sewing kit, a pair of surgical scissors and a razor knife, all of it covered in dried blood.

"Oh, dear God. Jesus," cried Private Investigator Jensen. "I'm going to be sick."

Sheriff Hanks and Deputy Steele turned in the direction of the Mustang. The open passenger door hid the kneeling detective. A moment later the private investigator bolted from behind the car door. He fell to the ground, puking violently.

Sheriff Hanks raced to the car. On the floor of the front seat, the lid of the cooler was upright. Inside the cooler were two chunks of packaged dry ice. Three plastic freezer bags were sitting on top of the ice, labeled in neat printing. Each of them contained an object about the size of a fist. The contents of the first two were dark brown, almost black. The object in the third package looked much fresher. Zeb had seen enough animal organs to recognize the size and shape of a heart. Silently he read the labels. Amanda Song Bird, 10/18/99. Angel Dablo Bright 10/18/92. The date on the package with Sara Winchester's heart was yesterday.

"Come on," said Sheriff Hanks. "We'd better have a look inside the Roadhouse. God knows what else we're going to find."

Walking past the open bathroom window of the bar, they heard a muffled voice. The sheriff sneaked a peak to see a man bound by both his hands and feet. A piece of duct tape was over his mouth.

"We got a live one," said Zeb. "Deputy Steele, check your weapon. Jensen, stay in the shed."

"I'm licensed to carry and conceal," said the private detective. "And I am."

"Back us up then, but keep your weapon out of sight. I don't want you drawing down on anyone unless it's a matter of life and death."

The lock on the cellar door of the Roadhouse was rusted. Sheriff Hanks broke it open by smashing a rock against it. Once inside, the trio sneaked up the back stairwell. The only sound inside the bar was the muffled cry of the gagged man in the bathroom. Once certain there was no one else present, they untied the man and helped him into the bar area.

"It's about fucking time you got here. I could've died," shouted the man.

"Who are you?" asked the sheriff.

"Billy Belton, Billy Ray Belton" the man replied.

"What are you doing here?"

"I'm the fucking bartender, you jackass. I work here."

"What happened?"

"I got smacked in the back of the head. Look it. I've got a goose egg the size of a, hell, the size of a goose egg. I need a fucking shot of whiskey."

The man poured himself three fingers of booze and downed it with the flick of a wrist and tip of the head.

"Christ almighty, my head hurts."

"Who did this to you?" asked Zeb. "Were you robbed?"

"I don't think so, but there was a kidnapping."

"What are you talking about?" asked the sheriff.

"Red Doerry, the owner. They tied him up and took him."

"Who tied him up? Who took him?"

"Two old guys. One loco Indian and one crazy cowboy. I don't know who the hell they were, but Red sure as shit did. I never seen people with murder in their eyes like that before. I'm damn lucky I'm not dead. I can tell you this. Those two are fixin' to kill Red, no doubt about it."

"Fuck! God damnit!" Zeb pounded his fist on the bar and pointed a finger at the bartender. "Did they say anything that might tell you where they took him?"

"They didn't say shit that made any sense,'" he replied. "But I'm gonna sue the bastards and the county and the goddamn Indian tribe to boot. Screw all of 'em. And I wanna swear out an assault complaint against those two old bastards that banged me over the head. They tried to kill me."

"What did they say? Repeat it for me, even if it doesn't make sense to you."

"I ain't sayin' a word until I talk to an attorney."

Zeb reached across the counter and grabbed the man by the open neck of his shirt and lifted him off the floor.

"Don't piss me off. I'm in no mood. What did they say?"

The man's face turned red then blue as Zeb tightened his grip.

"Let me the fuck down and I'll tell ya'."

Zeb lowered him to the floor but maintained a tight grip around the man's neck.

"Take it easy, would ya', copper? They were talkin' trash, but it didn't amount to shit as far as I could tell."

"It might make sense to me. Right now I'm getting a little short on time. My temper isn't getting any longer either. Tell me what they said?"

"That old white guy, the one Red called Jake the Snake, said Red wasn't no better than his old man. He said Red's old man was burnin' in hell. And the Indian says burning in hell is too good for Junior's old man. Then Junior says to him, "I seen what you two done. I know what happened to my old man. You ain't foolin' me." That set both the old timers off something fierce."

"What do you mean?"

"The old Indian says to Red, "You're a lying sack of shit. You didn't see nothin. You don't know crap." Then Jake the Snake pulls out a gun he's got tucked in his belt, holds it up to Junior's ear and whispers something to him.""

"What did he say?"

"I couldn't make it out on account he was talking so quiet like, and I was scared shitless. I did catch one word. Iit sounded like boneyard. Then the cowboy, he smacks Red with the butt end of the pistol and tells the Indian to tie him up with his hands behind his back. When they got Red all tied up, he yells at me to turn around and lay on the floor. I'm figurin' that I'm a dead man. I'm thinkin' my fuckin' brains are gonna' get blown out the back of my head. So I start to run, but as quick as I lit out, I saw stars and everything went black. Next thing I know I wake up with a knot on the back of my head the size of a baseball. Fuck it. I'm gonna sue everybody in sight. I ain't gonna go through this kind of shit without ending up a rich man. I know my rights. I'm even gonna make sure I get on the TV news. I know just the lawyer to call."

"Shut up, you fucking moron," shouted Zeb.

"You think by boneyard he meant the graveyard up in Morenci?" asked the detective.

Zeb knew exactly what Jake meant, and it wasn't the graveyard. But this was the perfect way to get the private detective out of his hair. If this thing was going down the way Zeb thought it might, he sure as hell didn't need any witnesses. He found lying to the detective easy.

"It's either there, or if Jake is really twisted, maybe he's taking him to his granddaughter's grave. You head up to Morenci. If you see anything, call me. Don't try and be a hero. Deputy Steele, secure everything in the shed. Also, see what else you can find in the bar."

"Where are you going?" asked Deputy Steele.

"I'm going back into town to see if anybody saw them. I got a pretty good idea where they were when they hatched this little plan."

"What about me?" asked the bartender.

"Call your frickin' attorney," said the sheriff. "He'll tell you what to do."

"Good idea," said the bartender.

The sheriff and Deputy Steele watched Detective Jensen's car speed north toward Morenci.

"You know they didn't go to Morenci," said Deputy Steele, "don't you?"

Zeb nodded solemnly. He stepped into the cab of the Dodge Dakota and headed onto the main highway. Outside of Safford, as the scenery opened to cotton fields and broad expanses of desertscape, the sheriff's heart began to race. The speedometer was pushing one hundred and ten when he eyed the County Road 6 turnoff ahead in the distance. He slowed and signaled a left turn to Hell Hole Canyon. The boneyard, as Jake called it, the Apache burial grounds, was a legendary spot Zeb had never set foot in and for good reason. Not only was it sacred territory to the Apaches, the rattlesnake dens were incredibly dangerous.

Years earlier, in an offhanded conversation, Jake had told Zeb that Hell Hole Canyon was the one spot in Graham County where hidden secrets would remain buried for time and all eternity. The sheriff knew this was where he would find Jake, Song Bird and Red Junior.

The western portion of County 6 was rough, deeply rutted and hard going, making it impossible to move along faster than twenty miles an hour. The highway department treated it as a seasonal road, grading it twice a year. From the looks of it, this wasn't the season. Freshly disturbed dirt and a clean set of tire tracks told him someone had passed by here very recently. Ahead of him the road twisted in a series of switchbacks and lost elevation rapidly as it descended toward the canyon. If Jake and Song Bird were even just a half mile ahead of him, they couldn't be seen. If they had ditched their vehicle and were moving on foot, he might never see them.

As the high desert gave way to canyon land, Zeb found himself in the rare low desert forest. High cottonwoods and mesquite trees covered a layer of agave and golden barrel cacti and a sweeping sea of red grass. Within another mile, the density of the trees formed a canopy over the road. Red deer scooted across the dirt path. A family of ring-tailed possums stopped playing to eye his passing. After crossing a couple of creek beds, Zeb found himself in a dead-end canyon. He turned off the truck and listened. It was quiet except for the shrill squawking of a pair of high-flying turkey buzzards. When they disappeared over a high canyon wall, it was just Zeb and stillness until he heard a faint, distant shout. He stepped out of the cab and walked the base of the canyon wall. Hidden behind a series of large boulders was Jake's car. Following along the soft stone, he spied a small break in the rocks. He pulled back some brush and spotted what looked like a small cave. He ran back to the truck and grabbed a flashlight and an extra bullet clip.

Tugging his hat down firmly on his head, Zeb crept into the cave on his hands and knees. The sandy floor had been recently disturbed. Three sets of hand and boot prints were everywhere. Staying very low he crawled for a hundred feet until the cave opened up, and he had plenty of room to stand. In the near distance a small stream of sunlight appeared. His eyes slowly adjusted to the dark. He could see that the walls of the cavern were covered with petroglyphs.

Outside in the sunlight, he could hear the voices of men talking angrily. He edged along the wall of the cave. Near the entrance, he peered around the corner, gun drawn. It was Jake, Song Bird and Red Junior. Song Bird's back faced Zeb, but he could see Jake's face plainly as he held Red Junior close to the ground, pistol pressed tightly against the back of his neck.

"Look, you little bastard. My trigger finger has got one hell of an itch going."

"Noooo!" cried Red. "You can't do this. It's murder."

"No, it's not," said Song Bird. "It's the way things must be. We are putting things back into balance."

"Is this where you killed my father?" growled Red. "Is this where you took him that night?"

Jake loosened his grip. Red's face carried the expression of a death row inmate who had just been granted a reprieve.

"What do you know about that?" asked Jake.

"I was hiding in the back of the bar when you two took my old man away that night. I ducked down when I saw you had your guns drawn. If I had been packing heat, it would be the two of you, and not my old man, that's dead."

"You saw us take him?" asked Song Bird.

"Damn right I did, Chief. I saw everything you rat bastards did."

"Your father was a killer and a rapist," said Jake. "The way he died was too good, even for the likes of him."

"He raped our daughters and killed a dozen people from my reservation," said Song Bird.

"Your daughters were whores," shouted Red. "And those Injuns we killed were all a bunch of losers who deserved to die."

Jake pushed the bound man back to the desert floor and ground the heel of his boot against his neck. Song Bird kicked the downed man in the ribs, hard, twice.

"You never answered my question, you bastards. Is this where you killed my father?"

Jake slipped the gun back into his pants, grabbed the scruff of Junior Parrish's neck and dragged him to the edge of a shallow, abandoned well that had long ago become a rattlesnake den.

"Take a look for yourself. That's what's left of him, right there."

Red Junior retched and began to spit venom.

"You bastards. I'm going to kill the both of you, if it's the last thing I do."

"You're runnin' out of time for that," said Jake. "Cause you're just about to join your old man."

Sheriff Hanks chambered a bullet and flipped the safety to off. Stepping out of the cave into the light, he shouted.

"Hold it right there, Jake, Song Bird, Junior. Nobody moves."

Song Bird and Jake froze. A mockingbird, hissing like a snake, zipped over their heads in a low flying trajectory. Red Junior cackled.

"Jake, mind telling me what the fuck is going on here?"

The retired sheriff took a single stride toward the current one.

"You can tell it from there. I can hear you fine. Stay where you are and keep your hands in front of you. I know you're carrying a gun in the back of your belt."

"Zeb," said Jake. "I always knew there would come a day when you were going to have to grow up and see the world as it really is. I just didn't think it would be under circumstances like this."

"Like you always said, Jake. Things happen the way they do for a reason."

"That they do, Zeb. And when I'm through talkin', I betcha a plate of donuts you're gonna understand my point of view. If the chips fall where I think they will, you might even see it my way."

"I doubt it," said Zeb. "But keep talking anyway. This story just keeps getting better and better."

"It's still one you can walk away from," said Song Bird,

ing Zeb by the Athabascan nickname he had given him in
childhood.

"Not a chance. Not while I'm still the law in this neck of the
woods. Go on, Jake. Let's hear your explanation."

Jake pointed into the rattlesnake pit.

"Those bones in there belong to Red Parrish Senior. He died
from a few too many snakebites."

"I don't suppose you expect me to believe he just stumbled
in there, do you?" asked Sheriff Hanks.

"If it would make things easier on you, you can believe
anything you want. But the truth is I threw him in there. Song
Bird helped me."

"Why?"

"He was a killer and a rapist. He killed a dozen or more
Apaches."

"How?"

"You know that bus stop out in front of the Roadhouse?"

"I know it."

"Do you? Think about it. Put yourself at the bus stop, sitting
on the bench, facing the road. Now think about what's
behind you."

Zeb could picture it in his mind as if he were there. He had
been there only hours earlier, but nothing had changed at Red's
Roadhouse since he went there as a kid. The front of the roadhouse was windowless. A small road from the parking lot led to
Red's shed. The shed had an office at the front with a small
window that looked directly over the bus stop. Inside that office,
Red kept a collection of rifles and shotguns.

"You're telling me that Red was using Indians for target
practice?"

"That's right," said Jake. "Any opportunity Red had to sight in
his hunting rifle on some poor bastard, he'd do just that. I'm
kind of disappointed you and your detective buddy didn't put it

together when he told you about the relationship between the missing persons cases and the bus stop at Red's."

"But he said the bodies were all found in Phoenix and Tucson."

"Shoot 'em, mutilate 'em and throw 'em in the trunk. Drive to the big city and dump 'em in bad neighborhoods, maybe even plant some drugs on 'em. Old Red was a planner."

"Why'd he do it?"

"He hated Indians. He hated our ceremonies and our religion," said Song Bird. "Not much more to it than that and an evil streak that ran real deep."

"We killed those dirty Injuns cause they're nothin' but a bunch of thievin' bastards," shouted Junior. "Every one of them dead assholes we caught stealin' from our place. Hell, I was only twelve when daddy paid me my first bounty on one of 'em. I wanted to scalp them, but the old man said no. He said that's what Injuns did."

Song Bird turned and kicked Junior in the face.

"Hold it, Song Bird," said Zeb. "Take it easy."

"You're fucking crazy, you good for nothin' Redskin," shouted Red Junior. "I *will* scalp you."

"Zeb, you want a piece of him?" asked Song Bird. "I'll hold him down for you."

"I don't want a piece of anything," replied Zeb.

"You will," said Jake.

"What's that supposed to mean?"

"You remember when you, Jenny and Amanda used to go out to Red's back in high school. The three of you would get all liquored up? I knew all about it even then. I should have stopped it, but I didn't."

It had never been spoken about between the men, and both of the girls promised never to tell their fathers that they had gone there with Zeb.

"Yeah, I remember."

"Well because of those little escapades, Red Senior got to know Jenny and Maya a little better than he should have. Over the years, he'd slip them drugs when they were drinking and rape them when they passed out," said Jake.

A horrible thought went through Zeb's mind. Could the grandchildren of both Jake and Song Bird have been conceived in rape? The idea sent his mind reeling. Had Red Junior, in some sort of twisted revenge for his father's death, killed his half-sisters?

"Don't tell me Red Senior was the father of Angel and Amanda?"

"Just Amanda," said Jake. "Angel..."

Jake paused, his eyes reddening with the pain of memory.

"What is it, Jake? Spit it out. Let's have the whole damn truth."

"Angel..."

Jake's voice choked as he spoke.

"Angel was your child."

Zeb's flesh rippled as a thousand thoughts detonated in his mind. He saw red. Then his vision turned as black as a starless, moonless night. The rest of the world crumbled into a million fragments and disappeared. His mind was left with but a single image, a mutilated child, Angel, his mutilated child, his unknown child mutilated.

The pain contracting in his gut forced him to bear down hard to keep from exploding. But the agony of his vision was too powerful. His knees buckled. He fell to the ground. It was useless to try and push the image from his thoughts. It took every ounce of what he had in him to remember he was the sheriff of Graham County. He was the law. The devious laughter spewing forth from Red Junior made his hatred rise. He forced himself to remember who he was and what he represented.

"How do you know for sure?" asked Zeb.

"Jenny told me," said Jake. "And she wrote you a letter before she died. I've got it with me right now. I've been carrying it around for five years."

Jake reached toward his back pocket.

"Don't go for your gun, Jake. I'll shoot you if I have to."

Jake slowly put his hands in the air and turned around, exposing a 9mm pistol between his belt and shirt.

"It's in my right rear pocket. Get it yourself."

Zeb eyed Song Bird who was keeping close watch on the downed Red Junior. Approaching Jake, he pulled the gun from Jake's belt and threw it in the undergrowth. Sliding his fingers into Jake's jeans, he pulled out an envelope and slowly retreated.

The envelope was sweat stained. The writing on the cover was barely legible. *Dad, please give this to Zeb if anything ever happens to me. Jenny*

Zeb reached in the envelope and pulled out the letter.

Dear Zeb,

If you are reading this, it means I am in jail or dead. I've made such a mess of my life that if I am dead, I'm probably better off. This is very difficult, but there is something you have to know. God, it's killing me to write this. If the ink is smeared it's from my tears. There is no easy way to say this. Zeb, I am so sorry I never let you know. I should have told you before. My child was your child. Angel Bright was our child. Her real name should have been Angel Hanks. I was going to tell you when she died, but I couldn't find the strength. Oh, how I prayed to find a way to let you know. The pain was so horrible that I chose not to make you suffer. You see, Zeb, I always loved you. And I always will, no matter what.

All my love, Jenny

Zeb folded the letter, put it back in the envelope and slid it into his pocket. He pointed his gun toward Red Junior.

"Let him up," said Zeb.

Red Junior made his way to his feet.

"Did you kill Angel Bright and Amanda Song Bird and Sara Winchester?" asked Zeb.

Junior hurled a gob of spit in Zeb's direction.

"Fuck you, you Injun loving paper cowboy."

Zeb raised his weapon and pointed it at Junior's head.

"You did, didn't you?"

"So what if I did? You're going to kill me either way. Why should I give you the satisfaction of knowing? It's not like you even knew the kid. Some kind of a father you were."

"You did kill her, didn't you? And you killed Amanda and Sara and God knows how many Apaches."

"Go ahead and shoot, cowboy. You'll find out just how good it feels to kill somebody you hate. But let me tell you something else."

Zeb lowered the gun and pointed it at Junior's heart. The weapon was practically weightless in his grip. His aim had never been sturdier or more true.

"Choose your words carefully, Junior. They're your last ones."

"You'll see my face every day for the rest of your life. It won't matter if you're dreaming or if you're awake, I'll be right there with you."

"You done talkin'?" asked Zeb.

"I enjoyed killing your daughter, your granddaughters. I'd do it again in a heartbeat."

"You're not going to get the chance," said Zeb.

The sheriff's finger squeezed the trigger so softly the recoil barely budged his arm. A single slug from his .357 penetrated the shirt, the flesh, the bone and then the organs of Red Parrish Junior. The second-generation murderer reeled backward in slow motion toward the rim of the rattlesnake pit. At the rim, he stumbled and reached out for Song Bird. The Medicine Man grasped the outstretched arm and used it as a lever to push Junior into the pit.

The three men, Jake, Zeb and Song Bird, listened to Red Junior's painful shrieks as they walked slowly to the edge of the pit. Red Junior's body lay directly on top of Red Senior's bones. A hundred hungry rattlers slithered over his dying body.

"True justice," said Jake, "has been served."

"Let's pray you're right," said Zeb.

EPILOGUE

Zeb took his usual seat at the back counter of the Town Talk. The past week had been a whirlwind. Breakfast, with a healthy dose of Doreen's special tenderness, would go a long way in easing the severe angst that permeated his every action.

Once word got out of that Michael Doerry was really Red Parrish Junior, convicted child pornographer and confessed killer of Angel Bright, Amanda Song Bird, Sara Winchester and a dozen or more Apaches, not a single person in town questioned Zeb's explanation of his death. There was universal agreement that such an easy death was too good for such a rotten human being.

Zeb, Jake and Song Bird decided to keep the story simple. After confronting Red Junior with the information they had pinpointing him as the killer of Angel Bright, Amanda Song Bird, and all the others, Red Junior drew a gun down on them. In self-defense, Zeb returned fire, killing him with a single bullet through the heart.

The men had hauled Red Junior's body from the snake pit to a more conspicuous spot behind the Roadhouse. Doc Yackley, who signed the death certificate, made no mention of the snakebites. A few days later the dead man was buried next to his father in the Morenci Graveyard. His tomb marked simply 'Junior Parrish'.

Throughout the county and across the reservation, Sheriff Zeb Hanks, ex-sheriff Jake Dablo and Medicine Man Jimmy Song Bird had become heroes. But Zeb couldn't shake the dishonesty and guilt he felt when one of the locals would pat him on the back and thank him for what he had done.

Zeb pondered his reflection in the mirror knowing it was impossible to tell the good guys from the bad ones.

Doreen brought him some fresh coffee. The black cloud hanging over the man she loved was unmistakable.

"What's goin' on here, sugar dumplin'? That long look on your face tells me you ain't quite so happy with the way this thing came out," she said.

"What's done is done," Zeb said. "Life must go on."

THE END

ALSO BY MARK REPS

ZEB HANKS MYSTERY SERIES

NATIVE BLOOD

HOLES IN THE SKY

ADIÓS ÁNGEL

NATIVE JUSTICE

NATIVE BONES

NATIVE WARRIOR

NATIVE EARTH

NATIVE DESTINY

NATIVE TROUBLE

NATIVE ROOTS (PREQUEL NOVELLA)

THE ZEB HANKS MYSTERY SERIES 1-3

AUDIOBOOK

NATIVE BLOOD

HOLES IN THE SKY

ADIÓS ÁNGEL

OTHER BOOKS

BUTTERFLY (WITH PUI CHOMNAK)

HEARTLAND HEROES

ABOUT THE AUTHOR

Mark Reps has been a writer and storyteller his whole life. Born in small-town southeastern Minnesota, he trained as a mathematician and chiropractor but never lost his love of telling or writing a good story. As an avid desert wilderness hiker, Mark spends a great deal of time roaming the desert and other terrains of southeastern Arizona. A chance meeting with an old time colorful sheriff led him to develop the Zeb Hanks character and the world that surrounds him.

To learn more, check out his website www.markreps.com, his AllAuthor profile, or any of the profiles below. To join his mailing list for new release information and more click here.

HOLES IN THE SKY - BOOK 2

Under the dimly lit sky, an effeminate hand gripped the shoulder of a nearly flaccid body and shook with unseeming strength. The clearing of a throat echoed in the otherwise silent night.

"You're still with me, aren't you, Padre? Padre!?"

The man, dressed in the collar of a Catholic priest, remained slumped over in the front seat of his station wagon. His nearly lifeless drooling lips pressed against the passenger window. His eyes stared mindlessly into a rapidly approaching oblivion. Any semblance of voluntary control was rapidly ebbing into an unholy blackness from which death could be his only escape.

"Last rites, Padre. Extreme Unction. How does the sound of that ring in your ears?

The religious man dug deeply into the last vestiges of his manhood. A vain attempt to curse his captor barely exuded from his dying lips.

With a stronger, more confident air, the captor spoke again. "Say that again, would you, Padre. I couldn't quite make it out."

A wheezing grunt oozed through his lips.

"Jesus sheds not a tear for a dying fool headed for hell."

The dying priest's stomach spasmed. A curdled glob of black and green fluid escaped unceremoniously through his flared nostrils. The driver shook his head in revulsion.

"Keep it together, Father. You're beginning to disgust me."

The watering eyes of the man in the collar disappeared somewhere deep into the back of his skull.

"What time frame does canon law prescribe as proper for the final sacrament?"

The sorrowful echo of the priest's unintelligible, dying voice volleyed around the inside of the car. The driver, stirred by its eeriness, grabbed the holy man by the collar and jerked him upright.

"Now listen up, Padre. About my religious-legal inquiry? Must Last Rites be administered within an hour of death? Or must the sacrament be administered prior to passing? If memory serves me correctly, I believe tradition demands the anointment of the dying must be administered before the soul departs the body. One of the great philosophical questions of all time, eh, Padre? Padre?"

The priest, held upright by a seatbelt, slumped limply forward in his seat. The man behind the wheel reached over, snatched the priest roughly by the hair and growled his question sternly.

"When precisely does the soul exit the body? Can you feel it leaving your body? More importantly, can you sense the direction its heading? Tell me, Padre, is your soul going to heaven or is it going to meet its doom in oblivion? If I were a gambler, I would put my money on hell."

The priest's strength had vanished. He could not even stir.

"Certainly the wise men in Rome who govern the Church have issued an edict or two on the subject."

The priest's corporal body collapsed into its final survival mode. He now breathed only the rasp of death.

"What? Speak up. You haven't answered my question. Maybe you don't have the answer? Don't worry. You will soon enough."

The driver pulled the car off the smooth pavement into a low wash. He parked behind a thicket of scraggly scrub brush and switched off the engine. Reaching over, he grabbed the priest's shoulder, shaking him violently. When the holy man failed to respond, the driver reached into the glove compartment. He removed a small vial. It was labeled 'Holy Water, Saint Barnabus Church'. The driver took a swallow, tipped his head back and gargled before spitting the liquid onto the face of the dying man. The barely conscious priest managed a small gurgle through purplish-blue, foam-covered lips.

"Stay with me now, palsy-walsy. The best, as they say, is yet to come."

"Where is your God now, Padre? Hiding in the bushes? Waiting to save you? Why don't you have a little look around? Maybe you can find Him for me."

Grabbing him by the clerical collar, the driver angrily twisted the priest's neck, giving him a complete scan of the surrounding area.

"Nope, I don't think so. Your Savior has left you on your own. God Almighty has abandoned you in your time of need. Irony? Fate? Your call, Padre."

The driver released the priest's neck from his grip. From behind the seat he extracted a pair of neatly folded surgical gloves and a miner's hat. Methodically, he checked the brightness of the hat's lamp before forcing it tightly on his head. Finger by finger he tightened the gloves snugly around his smooth, uncalloused hands.

"Now don't go away, Padre. I'll be right back. I promise."

The man hopped out of the priest's station wagon. Lowering the back gate, he grabbed the legs of a rocking chair. He grunted as he tugged hard on the wooden legs of the chair. He smacked the chair clumsily onto the ground. His eyes and ears suddenly tuned in to the surrounding night. Assured no one was approaching, he flicked on the helmet's light. He grabbed the rocker and fought clumsily through the underbrush. When he reached a previously chosen spot in the ditch, he relieved himself of the burden. He took a moment to catch his breath as he squinted long and hard down the vanishing roadway. Confidently, he ambled back to the car. He shouldered his prey using the adrenaline surge that comes with the power of death over life.

"I hope you're easier to wrangle than that goddamned rocker of yours."

The dying priest's stench-filled breath echoed shallowly in his captor's ear.

"What's that?" asked the man. "You're slurring your speech. Speak clearly if you expect to be spoken to."

Suddenly a rustling froze him like stone. It was only a night animal scurrying through the underbrush. A chuckle pursed his lips.

"The dark of night, Padre, is the time the devil collects his due. I don't need to tell you that. That's common knowledge to a man of the cloth, is it not?"

Carefully, he laid the nearly dead weight on the lip of the highway. He took extra caution to make certain the priest's head didn't smash against the pavement.

"Lucky you, Padre, the pavement is still warm. Let us call it my way of giving comfort to the dying. No one wants to die alone in a cold, hard bed."

The man retightened his gloves and glanced up beyond the

nearby peak of Mount Graham. The night sky was pregnant with a bounty of stars.

"It just doesn't get any more beautiful than this," he sighed. "Life is beautiful. And death, talk to me Father, is the Grim Reaper casting his shadow over you yet?"

Stepping down into the ditch, he grabbed the rocking chair and dragged it into the westbound lane. He triangulated with his hands to make certain the rocker was in the dead center of the lane.

"Fill in the blank for me, Padre. Death is...come on now. Death is...you know the answer. Death is...perfection," he sneered. "And, He is your next visitor."

Reaching under the unconscious priest's arms, he hoisted him into the chair. As the man stood back to survey his handiwork, he realized something was missing.

"Ah, yes. How silly of me."

His heart pitter-pattered with glee as he sprinted back through the underbrush to the station wagon. He reached under the seat.

"There you are. You little devil."

Dashing back through the arroyo, he emerged precisely where he had left his conquest.

"Here you go, Padre. Where you're going, you might want this."

He slipped the priest's personal Bible into bluish fingers.

"I understand Saint Peter is partial to those who cough up an entrance fee."

The rites of Extreme Unction were administered ritualistically. When the sacrament was fully dispensed, he kissed the priest on the forehead. With a smile, the blesser tipped the priest's head toward the heavens and hoarsely bellowed one final benediction.

"God, I know you are out there. I know you can hear me. Get ready. I am returning another sacrificial lamb to heaven's flock."

Having spoken his mind, the man trotted a half mile down the road where he had hidden his vehicle behind an abandoned gas station.

READ HOLES IN THE SKY NOW

Made in the USA
Middletown, DE
15 July 2019